3

MOE HOWARD
& THE 3 STOOGES

The
Pictorial
Biography
of the
Wildest
Trio
in the
History of
American
Entertainment

MOE HOWARD
&
THE 3 STOOGES
BY MOE HOWARD

CITADEL PRESS
Secaucus, New Jersey

Fourteenth printing

ISBN 0-8065-0554-0 (hardcover)
ISBN 0-8065-0723-3 (paperbound)

Published by
Citadel Press
A division of
Lyle Stuart, Inc.
120 Enterprise Ave.
Secaucus, N.J.

In Canada: Musson Book Company
A division of General Publishing Co. Limited
Don Mills, Ontario

Manufactured in the
United States of America by
Halliday Lithograph Corp.,
West Hanover, Mass.

Designed by
Peretz Kaminsky

**Library of Congress
Cataloging in Publication Data**

Howard, Moe
    Moe Howard & the 3 Stooges.

    Filmography: p.
    Includes index.
    1. Howard, Moe. 2. The Three Stooges.
3. Comedians—United States—Biography.
I. Title.
PN2287.H73A35
791.43′028′0924 [B] 76-58430

Acknowledgment

The publisher wishes to thank Alvin H. Marill
for his assistance in preparing the manuscript of
this book for publication.

Dedicated to my wonderful wife, Helen, and my son, Paul, who had confidence in my ability to write a book.

And to my darling daughter, Joan, without whose help there never would have been a book.

Contents

Childhood and the Early Years

THERE WAS LITTLE TO RECALL about baby Moses Harry Horwitz. Only that his dad intimated that he was an ugly infant, a sort of shriveled monkey. Dad should have kept that to himself, for he was reminded sharply and often by the tot's mother that he was no bargain either.

After three brothers (Irving, Jack, and Sam), I was to have been a girl, or so Jessup the butcher prophesied. And for the prediction I avoided his shop for years. Anyway, my mother conceded that if I wasn't a beautiful baby, then at least I'd turn out to be the smartest.

These memories were gleaned from bedtime stories my mother and father told me. Late at night I listened, enthralled, storing them all in my mind forever. And now, how easy for me to recall them in every detail.

When I was a little older I would stare into the mirror. Seeing my face covered with large jagged freckles, I realized my Dad was right. I would end up the ugly duckling of the Horwitz family. I soon discovered that those jagged freckles would stand me in good stead in the early 1900s.

When I was an infant I was always falling out of bed, over chairs, and off tables. I never cried, never broke any bones, never even had a black-and-blue mark. My parents and friends thought it was uncanny. I think it may have been an omen. I was about two when I did have my first real accident. My father had taken my brother Sam (who always was known as Shemp) and me for a walk down Cropsey Street in Ulmer Park, Brooklyn, near the picnic grounds. Shemp kept stopping to look into the penny picture machines. He seemed to always have pennies; I had my suspicion where he got them. I kept begging him for a peek and he finally boosted me up to the viewer and onto the metal foot rest provided so that small boys like me could be held up to watch the pictures flip by on cards. While Father had walked off to talk to another man, I was happily watching the peek-a-boo machine when a horse-drawn fire engine came roaring up the road, belching steam and clanging its bell. Shemp turned to watch and let go of me, leaving me hanging there. It seemed that I turned to take a look, too, lost my grip, and fell, hitting my nose on the corner of the foot rest. After over two years of falling off of everything without a scratch, I lay there on the ground, my face a bloody smear. My father saw me, ran up, and picked me up in his arms, tears streaming from his eyes down his fiery red moustache and into my face.

A crowd had gathered around us by then. Someone directed my father to a nearby doctor. Shemp followed close behind, yelping so loud you would have thought he was the one who was hurt. I could never forget sitting on the doctor's lap. He had a moustache and a Van Dyke beard, and although I had gone through so much, the shock could not equal the terrible breath that doctor kept blowing into my face as he mopped up the blood, took a needle out of a little brown jar, and began stitching my nose back on.

When my mother saw me she figured the worst had happened. She started to cry and that started Shemp yelping all over again. My brothers Irving and Jack had to yank him into another room with their hands clapped over his mouth. No one ever thought to ask how it had all happened and Shemp certainly wasn't going to tell. My mother finally calmed down and began taking things into her own efficient hands. Several days later I was smiling again. Taking a good look at me and noticing that my nose, which had been cut from one side to the other, was stitched on quite crooked, she was wild! She phoned the doctor, who rushed over and took the bandage off, cleaned up my nose a little, and prepared to put on another bandage. My mother came up alongside him and, before he knew what had happened, belted him twice over the head with a broom and kept swatting him, as she would a horsefly, all the way down the steps, yelling, "You ruined my son's face. You ruined him. You gave him a crooked nose."

Moe (front) at age three, with brothers Jack, Irving and Shemp.

Moe (second from left in top row)
and the Brooklyn P.S. 128
baseball team in 1913.

No one in our family or, for that matter, in our neighborhood, ever saw that doctor again. Later, we found out that he had been practicing in several areas without a license. My mother began looking all over for doctors. She was checking with everyone in the area when she found out about a Professor Beck who specialized in cases such as mine. His fee was fifteen dollars a visit and my mother figured she'd try one visit and test him out. How far a mother will go for the love of a son! Over the years my mother proved that there was no limit.

At this time my family had financial problems. How could my mother pay Professor Beck? I can see her now, taking her shiny copper frying pan from the kitchen wall and wrapping it in a piece of brown paper; then with the pan and me in her arms, she took the elevated train and streetcar up to Dr. Beck's office, where he put me on a little table and took off my bandage. He looked at my nose and clicked his tongue several times, explaining to my mother that he would have to take out the stitches and redo the whole job. I'm sure she expected as much.

After a few minutes of conversation, my mother had full confidence in Professor Beck. I was to come back every ten days for a reexamination. During the operation, which lasted about twenty minutes, my mother's head was bowed across my ankles; she was holding my legs and sobbing.

When it came time to pay the fee, my mother told Professor Beck that she had no money and asked him if he would accept the beautiful copper pan as payment. His eyes lit up. How was my mother to know that all the copper utensils that Dr. Beck's mother had left him and which he loved so much had been destroyed in a fire? He accepted it graciously, with the understanding that in exchange for every copper pot that my mother gave him for payment he would give her an enameled one so that she would have some kitchenware.

Seven visits and seven copper pots later, Dr. Beck told my mother the bad news. Due to ruptured eye nerves, I would temporarily lose my eyesight. My mother's face went pale and, after a speechless moment, she said, "So long as God has guided me to this office, things must turn out right." And they did, although I was blind for eleven months.

During this period, Shemp was at his mischievous worst, telling our parents that I was faking the loss of my sight and using it as a cover to spy on him. This was really laughable as it was around this time that Shemp had taken a liking to stuffing things into toilets and stopping them up.

By the time I was almost four I had perfect vision again. My nose was straight but scarred, and my hair had grown into a mass of beautiful long curls. They were to become the cause of most of my battles as a young boy.

Shemp was now five and a half, Jack was seven, and Irving was nine. Mother had won the battle with the school to let Shemp into kindergarten, and I was left at home. Being somewhat self-sufficient, I didn't mind making my own breakfast, washing dishes, or even helping my mother scrub floors. Shemp would tease me by saying, "Mother, where's the maid?" referring to me, of course. My mother would ask naïvely, "What maid?" Whereupon Shemp would reply, "The little maid with the *curls.* " Knowing that I had heard his comments, Mother would give him a half-hearted wack for his insults and he would laugh and run downstairs. I was hurt but not mad. Mother would kiss me and tell me not to mind Shemp, that Pa would fix him. But Pa never fixed anybody. He didn't have the heart to swat a mosquito—and there were plenty of them—let alone strike one of his sons.

So it was Mother who made all the financial plans, did all the managing, made all the clothes and meals. She did the laundry and cleaning with what little help I, as a four-year-old kid, could give. And she did all the punishing—what little there was of it. Pa was the boogie man that ma created, a boogie man who scared nobody.

Jack and Irving were model children—good students who did little odd jobs in the neighborhood to help with the family finances. Shemp, on the other hand, was an impossible crybaby, a stocking and pants destroyer, a general creator of disturbances. When chore time came, he would develop a stomach-ache, a headache, a toothache, or any old ache that would get him out of his share of work.

Curly as a teenager.

Moe's mother and father,
Jennie and Solomon Horwitz.

The school in Ulmer Park, where we lived, went only to the fifth grade. A student would have to go either to Coney Island (five miles away) or to Bensonhurst (four miles away) to continue school. My mother learned of a little section called Bath Beach in the Bensonhurst area, which housed the upper crust. She decided to scout around, making daily trips to Bath Beach and looking at different parts of the neighborhood each day. She found there were only six Jewish families in the area and no synagogue, but there was a streetcar line to Coney Island and an elevated structure which ran throughout Bath Beach. Mother would come home each afternoon exhausted from these scouting expeditions, but not too tired to make our evening meal. Then she would stay up until all hours of the night, washing, ironing, knitting, and making lunches for school the next day.

Many times while lying on my mattress on the floor, I could see my mother nodding during her work. Shemp would be sleeping alongside my father, snoring louder than anyone I've ever heard. Often I would tiptoe in the room and touch my mother on the arm when she started to doze. She would look up and smile and carry me back to bed. She had terrific stamina for a woman only slightly over five feet tall. It was incredible, for she never complained. She would make all the decisions concerning the family without consulting anyone, and one day without a word spoken we found ourselves moving to Bath Beach.

It cost us eleven dollars to move our things to our new home. On moving day I came down with a very special variety of mumps, the kind that swell inward. The type that required an operation by Dr. Beck in New York. This time my mother paid twelve dollars, *cash!*

Sitting by an open window, one summer's day in 1901, we Horwitz brothers were at the mercy of the mosquitoes. Like everyone else, we were burning punk, a concoction on a little red stick that smoked like old rags. Punk was a Chinese invention for lighting firecrackers and its smell made the one who was burning it as sick as it made the mosquitoes. The swamps in the area bred thousands of malaria-carrying mosquitoes. It wasn't until years later that they finally filled the swamps in. This year Mother, who had begun dabbling in real estate, had made several good commissions, and Dad was still bringing in a little as a clothing cutter. That day we all decided to go out on our first picnic to a place called West Farms in New York. We were preparing to eat lunch when Shemp, who already had eaten, scooped up a handful of my tomatoes and disappeared. A short time later, a man from a nearby family gathering came over to our group dragging a screaming Shemp by the ear. The man, with tomatoes dripping over face and clothes, was shaking Shemp like a rag doll. Infuriated, my mother jumped up and hit the man with her sun umbrella and a free-for-all resulted. It was madness! When it was over, my father was lying against a tree with a bloody nose, my mother was swinging the closed umbrella in every direction, Irving was crying in the grass, and Shemp sat there screaming like a person being strangled although there was no one within ten feet of him. I had been hit by assorted chinaware and sat there wondering what it was all about. None of us had a clean spot left on our previously clean suits. When all the confusion died down, Shemp got the beating of his life in front of the stranger. The man, Mr. Mitchell, apologized for shaking Shemp. My mother apologized for hitting Mr. Mitchell. We found out later that my father's bloody nose came from my mother's umbrella. Our adventure led to Mr. Mitchell's becoming our friend, eventually moving into the Bath Beach neighborhood and becoming a partner with my mother in many of her real estate ventures.

Irving was seven and entered P. S. 101 in Bath Beach. He always attended and was average at everything. Jack was quite bright and took his studies in stride. At that time there were no junior high schools. You spent eight years in grade school and if you graduated you went directly on to high school. Both Irving and Jack graduated and went on. Shemp started school in 1901 at the age of six. In his first few years at school he barely squeezed his way through each level.

My school career began in September 1903, when I was six. Whenever I attended school—which in later years wasn't very often—I was constantly fighting. I fought on my way to school, in school, and on my way home. As I said before, my hair had grown very long, and every school day I would awaken a half hour before everyone else so my mother could wind finger curls through my hair; they reached almost to my shoulders. There were about twenty of them in all and resembled a bunch of cigars stuck on my head. Knowing that it was my mother's greatest delight to spend that half hour arranging my curls, I didn't complain. But soon it became the battle of my school career. (A short time later, my youngest brother Jerome, better known as "Curly," was born—I called him "Babe"—another boy who was to have been a girl. I kept hoping he'd have curly hair, so that much of my mother's attention would fall on him. No such luck, though; he had long, straight, brown hair.) From the first days of walking to school with Shemp, I would have to grit my teeth and take the teasing remarks from both boys and girls, but I believe that I started planning my revenge on the very first day. I remember the look on the face of Mrs. Lynch, the principal, when she first saw me. She called to her assistant and said smilingly—I'm certain they were both holding back hysterical laughter—"Meet Moses Horwitz, our new student with the beautiful hair."

As she played with one of my curls, she instructed her assistant to take me to the kindergarten to meet Mrs. Warner. I think she wanted to call me "girl" but chose "child" instead. If she had, I might never have gone to school at all. Even at my tender age I was a stubborn kid. Fortunately for me the schools were coeducational, and Mrs. Warner was kind and intelligent. She sat me in the first row of boys adjoining the last row of girls, right next to a girl who had curls longer than mine. I was grateful for her consideration but my fighting began early in kindergarten, and I fought from then until I was eleven. I sported more black eyes and bloody noses than any youngster alive . . . anywhere. My mother never knew the real cause of my shiners and bloody noses for I told her I had gotten them from accidents at play, and Mrs. Warner could never convince her that I should have a regular boy's haircut. I knew I must give my mother her half hour of pleasure even if it meant that I had to throw punches at everyone, no matter what the result—and most of the time I gave a pretty good account of myself.

Kindergarten was just not for me. I raised hell from the start. Sometimes I fought about my curls, sometimes I just raised hell. One of my worst offenses was dipping little spitballs into the ink-

At Coney Island in 1914. Moe behind the wheel, Jack behind him, Shemp on the right.

well and blowing them at different kids in the room. One time I put red ink in my mouth, laid my head on the desk, and let the blood-colored ink ooze out. I must have been convincing, for it really scared the teacher and the students. Finally the principal was called in—my parents, too. The kids and I had a good time of it but I paid for it later.

It seemed my school-days fighting career was endless. Finally the principal could stand it no longer and moved me from P. S. 101 to P. S. 128. The change made no difference except that there I met a freckle-faced redhead appropriately named Rusty. His red hair had eyebrows to match and his freckles were not at all like mine, which he called "ginger snaps." I was the only boy, I think, who had black hair, black eyebrows, blue eyes, *and* a face full of freckles. Rusty and I became inseparable friends. He would wait for me after school and we would walk home together—he believed there was safety in numbers. Now, when the other boys would call me sissy or "girly-girly," he would feel sorry for me, and whenever my opponent was too big to handle, he'd join in. We would stand back to back fighting three boys at a time, and soon Rusty was getting his share of black eyes and bloody noses. When I got my boxing gloves, Rusty and I practiced together every day preparing for our daily fights at school. Rusty liked me . . . curls and all.

When I was ten, I began to notice girls and had finally figured out that the bumps under sweaters weren't hidden grapefruit. Now they were something to be admired, at least at a distance. Shemp, with his freckles, good humor, and wiliness, was becoming increasingly popular and was finally emerging from his whimpering stage.

I was still fighting my way through school when the principal sent for my father. My parents hadn't yet realized that my long curls were causing most of the trouble. I realized they were very upset, so for the next semester, I took all the jibes without return fire. Rusty thought there was something wrong with me. For the next couple of years I shied away from trouble, I went to school early, scurrying through the basement to class, and afterward I hid in the engineer's room until everyone was gone and then I would sneak home. My parents found out about my shortcuts and threatened to send me to another school. The thought of being chided by another group of kids who had never seen my crop of curls kept me in school—suffering. It wasn't so much taking the ribbing as it was the possible loss of my chum Rusty.

Another of our buddies was Donald McMann, who had recently moved to the neighborhood. We met on his first day at my school. He was walking to one side of me as we headed for school and I could see he was appraising me from head to toe, perhaps trying to figure out what sort of freckle-faced freak I was. Don had just turned ten and was about an inch and a half taller than I and maybe seven or eight pounds heavier—and strong. He had black hair, black eyes, and a face as dark as a black man. He kept in step with me and eyed me all the way to the vacant lot which opened up to the entrance of the school.

When we got to the center of the lot, there stood the guy everyone in school called "Ugly." He was mean and ugly and caused me no end of trouble during the last semester. He saw me and shouted, "Hey! Millie, I'd like to screw you tonight, can I have a date? Hey, what happened to your tits?" Normally, I would have lit into him. Instead, I was more embarrassed at what this dark, handsome new boy would think than anything else, and thoughts of trouble in a new school turned in my mind.

Then I heard Don speak for the first time, a low, distinct voice trembling with excitement. "Did you hear what that monkey said?"

"Yes," I nodded. To speak would have brought me to tears.

"Aren't you gonna do anything?" Words wouldn't come; I shook my head no!

Ugly spoke again. "Your whole family are Jew sissies." Like a cannon blast, Don leaped at him and with one punch knocked him to the ground He lay there silently. Donald opened his lunch box, took out a Thermos of cold milk, poured it on his handkerchief, and mopped Ugly's brow until he came to. He pulled that ugly clown to his feet and then made him kneel and, in front of about eight boys and six girls, made him apologize to me. I wanted to run, and would have if Don hadn't held me and whispered, "You meet me by the drinking fountain after school." I wished I could tell him why I didn't punch that ugly creep all over the lot, but I just couldn't. Meanwhile word had spread all over school about how the handsome newcomer had flattened Ugly.

After school, Don took Rusty and me to his house. In his room, the walls were covered with pictures of fighters: Billy Papke, Fighting Dick Nelson, Bob Fitzsimmons, Jeffries, Corbett, and others. There were all sizes of dumbbells spread out on the floor and a pair of boxing gloves hung nearby.

Moe's mother, Jennie Horwitz.

I gazed into Donald's mirror and saw my curls hanging down, a good ten inches long. I glanced over at Donald and Rusty, two normal-looking young boys. I looked in the mirror again and then something on Don's dresser caught my eye. A shiny object with black enamel handles. I looked at myself again, trying to create one last impression.

I grabbed the scissors and, with my eyes closed, began to circle my head, clipping curls all the way around. I didn't dare to look at the floor to see what had fallen. When I finished, I dropped the scissors, afraid to look at myself. Tears quietly flowed down my cheeks.

When I finally opened my eyes, I found Rusty and Don pointing at me and laughing hysterically. I couldn't resist looking into the mirror. I choked up. There wasn't a laugh in me. There in the mirror I caught sight of the haircut that was to make me famous in the 1920s. I laughed, then I cried, and I shuddered seeing all those curls lying on the floor and realizing that I had destroyed one of my mother's few pleasures.

I turned and ran out of the house. I hid in a nearby barn where I stayed until dark; then I moved underneath our porch. I lay in the dirt and shivered until midnight and, from outside, I could hear my mother sobbing and my father describing me to the police: long black curls . . . a mass of freckles . . .

At about two in the morning, shaking with chills and saddened by the weeping of my mother on the porch above, I knew I had to give myself up. I coughed softly a couple of times, then I coughed a bit louder. "I think Moe is under the porch," said my father, grabbing a candle and bringing it out to the lattice. He pulled it aside, peered in and, speaking softly so he wouldn't frighten my mother, urged me to come out. Shemp knelt alongside my father. He wouldn't dare go under the porch even in the daytime. My father finally crawled in while Shemp held the candle. I assured my dad that there was nothing wrong with me. He let me know I had scared my mother out of her wits, for which I was sorry, but he didn't notice my shorn head in the dark. We all walked onto the porch and then into the lighted hallway.

My brother Shemp spotted me first. He let out a war whoop. "Take a look at your son with the fright wig. He thinks it's Halloween, and what do you know, it's not a wig: it's a brand new haircut." Then Mother, Irving, and Jack came in. They stared speechless for a moment. Then Mother looked at me. I looked at her and the tears welled up in my eyes, then the tears welled up in hers. She said softly, "Thank God you did it. I didn't have the courage."

My grades in school were always excellent. I never had to take my books home to do my homework as I had such a retentive memory that I could absorb everything right in class. But the grief I gave my teachers far outweighed the joy of my scholarship. On Friday afternoons, when we students would be taking our tests, I would finish long before the others. There was nothing to do but listen to those forty pens scratching on paper. I had to do something, so I would let out a war whoop like the bloodcurdling cry of some savage Indian. Almost automatically, the teacher would yell, "Moses, into the cloakroom!" One time I remember, I peeked around the corner of the cloakroom and asked the teacher if I could go to the lavatory.

"No! Get back in that cloakroom!" she yelled. I really had to go, so I peed in a flower pot. I soon found out that flower pots had drainage holes in them, and a clear yellow liquid ran out of the bottom, along the floor under the cloakroom door and into the classroom.

Show Biz via Vitagraph and the Melodrama

IT WAS 1908 and it was the year that I made up my mind that I was going to be an actor. I was eleven now and we had moved from Bath Beach.

In early spring of that year I attended school only 40 days out of a possible 103. Absent cards were constantly being mailed to our house. I'd wait for them to come and take them as soon as the postman put them in the box. Then I would forge a note that Moses was attending school in his grandmother's neighborhood. This routine worked for one entire semester and I'm sure my teachers didn't miss me.

During this period I had an awful time with the truant officers; fortunately in those days they had to ride in horse-drawn carriages so they had a hard time keeping up with me. They were now beginning to question my mother. She wanted no trouble; she was having enough of her own, so she lied for me. She said I had an aunt in New York who was desperately ill and alone and that I was the only one who could care for her.

While the truant officers were busy searching for me, I would be out catching frogs at a nearby pond, and selling them to a local saloon at fifteen cents apiece or a dollar for ten. I'd give seventy cents to my mother and spend the other thirty cents to go to the theater—a dime for train fare, a dime for lunch, and a dime to sit in the upper gallery of the melodrama theater. (Thirty cents for the orchestra, twenty cents for the balcony, and ten cents to sit close to heaven.)

My routine when I saw shows was to select an actor I liked best in the first act and follow him right through the play, disregarding all the other performers. I felt as if I *was* the performer. I lost myself completely. That night in bed I would recite the lines I remembered and I'd fall asleep dreaming I was playing the part. From 1908 to 1910 I probably saw sixty or seventy dramatic plays.

It was a half hour's ride from my home to the Brooklyn Vitagraph Studio on Avenue M and East 16 Street. Early in May 1909, I first approached the guard at the gate and asked if there were any actors who might want someone to run errands. One nice old gent, an Irish man with a brogue you could cut with a knife, spoke to me. "I'll be doin' the best I can for you, my buckaroo. Be patient and hang around with your book. God help us, there should be plenty for you to do around here." Within an hour "Old Dennis" got me an order for two newspapers: the New York *World* and *Billboard* magazine, a ham and egg sandwich, and a cup of coffee to be poured into John Bunny's own cup. I had completed my first mission and decided I would refuse any tips I was offered.

"You're daft," Dennis would say.

"Maybe," I replied. *It worked!*

Maurice Costello was one of the first to become curious. "Are you the lad that takes no money for his efforts?"

"Yes, sir!"

"Why?" he asked.

"Beccause I'm looking for a job in films."

He stared at me awhile and then said, "Come with me, I want you to meet someone . . . now, don't be scared."

How could I be scared when everything was working out so perfectly?

He took me to an office and introduced me to a man who looked like Foxy Grandpa in the old Sunday comic strip. "Van, I want you to meet a *good friend* of mine," Mr. Costello said, and then turned back to me and asked, "Uh . . . lad, what is your name?" Van began to laugh.

"Harry," I said.

Mr. Costello spoke again. "Van, I'm sure you can find a spot for my *cousin Harry* in your next film."

"I'm certain I can; even if he isn't your cousin, he has a wonderful face and would look well alongside Ken."

This man was Van Dyke Brooks, director of the film *We Must Do Our Best,* starring teenage Kenneth Casey. I said that I would leave my salary up to Mr. Costello, who piped up, "You see, Van, I'm Harry's agent." I thanked Mr. Costello profusely and told him I would still run errands for him, still with "no tips." We parted laughing, my head in the clouds.

Usually I was typecast as a street urchin or ragamuffin. My first film role took place in an orphanage in Bath Beach. I was the "bad boy," the typical bully-type, pushing kids around, forcing my way into their games, and winding up in a fist fight with the star.

Moe and Shemp, vaudevillians, in 1919.

I was soon appearing in films with John Bunny, Flora Finch, Earle Williams, Maurice Costello, Herbert Rawlinson, and Walter Johnstone, and when I wasn't acting with them, I was running their errands. Everything was so much simpler in filmmaking then. The scripts could hardly be considered more than bare outlines. The prop man took care of nearly everything: special effects, set dressing, powder work; he was the painter, carpenter, and electrician. Even the director and actors would occasionally lend a hand. Everyone was part of the general effort. You seldom heard the word *budget* mentioned. When expenses were running high, an impromptu meeting was held and corners were cut: less lavish costumes, or fifty extras instead of a hundred.

The team of Flora Finch and John Bunny made some very successful comedies. Flora was five foot nine and weighed 150 pounds. John was five four and 225. In three of their pictures, I played a street urchin, a very scholarly boy in another, and in one a hateful little snob. And because the directors found me versatile, I also had some interesting parts in three Maurice Costello films and played some nice bits with Earle Williams, a favorite juvenile of the day. Even Lillian Walker, a Vitagraph glamour girl, requested me for one of her films.

At the time, I was reluctant about mentioning to anyone—especially my family—that I was working in pictures. I must have started living my film parts, though, and it wasn't long before Irving, Jack, and Shemp began looking at me as if I was going nuts. Even my mother began to worry that there was something wrong with me.

I first met Ted Healy in July 1909. Rusty Johnson, Donald McMann, and I were virtually living on the beach. My uniform for sand and surf was my bathing suit and my ukulele that I played not well but loud. My voice wasn't too bad, the ukulele playing not too good; somehow, though, the combination worked. Everyone would gather around on the sand and join in singing. Even the older folks sitting some distance away would come in on the choruses. On the Saturday of the July 4th weekend, I heard a new voice among the singers on our beach, a loud rich voice. I followed the direction of the voice, and it was my first meeting with Ted, then using his christened name of Charles Ernest Lee Nash. Ted was about twelve, tall for his age. We were both singing the same song, "Oh, You Beautiful Doll," with me edging closer to him, hoping that his dynamic voice would drown out my poor ukulele efforts.

In our first talks I learned that his family spent the summer in the exclusive Wawanda Cottages near the beach, which meant that they were well enough endowed with wordly goods. I told him my name was Moe Horwitz, and he told me to call him Lee Nash. I was Jewish, he Scotch-Irish.

Along with a glib tongue and a lively personality, Lee Nash had strong ambitions toward being a successful businessman in his native Texas. The days of the entertainment world and an international career under the name of Ted Healy seemed far away. We became inseparable friends and, later, joined forces for one of the most enduring acts in show business history. At the end of the summer, I went back to Bensonhurst and Lee to his folks' Riverside Drive apartment in Manhattan.

In the summer of 1912, Ted's ideas of entering the business world faded for the moment and he, Rusty, Donald, and I became part of the Annette Kellerman Diving Girls; yes, girls. There were six girls and we four boys. We did a thirty-foot dive into a tank seven feet long, seven feet wide, and seven feet deep. We wore long bathing suits, the one-piece variety, with balls of crumpled newspaper stuffed in the breast area. After each dive, these paper falsies would drop down around our middles and we had to stay down in the water until we could push them back up where they belonged. Our careers with Annette Kellerman lasted only one season; we quit after one of the divers, a pretty young lady named Gladys Kelly, misjudged the tank and landed on the artificial waves made of papier-mâché and two-by-fours that decorated the side of the tank. She had broken her neck and was killed instantly.

Moe (second left) and Shemp (second right) with the Marguerite Bryant Players Stock Company, 1919.

Ted and I loved to play tennis at the Wawanda Cottages. He was tall and rangy and had a tremendous serve with which he continually beat the pants off me. The one sport in which I excelled was the hundred-yard dash. As tall as Ted was and as long as his legs were, there wasn't a time that I didn't beat him by at least a yard or more. He never got over this. He couldn't understand how a guy that was so short could run so fast.

By now you must realize I thought of Ted Healy as a brother. We had such terrific times together—sheer joy. It makes me sad now remembering how he turned on me in later years. I want to believe it was the liquor and that he didn't realize what he was doing.

One balmy summer's night in 1913, Shemp, Bob Woodman, Willie O'Connor, and I walked out of the theater with our dates near the beach in Bensonhurst.

We strolled along the sandy beach trying to talk our dates into skinny-dipping. We had almost persuaded them when Shemp whispered, "Fellows, I have a terrible cramp and if you don't mind I'll have to go under the boardwalk and relieve myself." To get under the boardwalk you had to stoop down and keep your head low. Shemp ducked under and that was the last we saw of him for forty-five minutes.

Only hours later did we learn what had happened. He had worked his way pretty far under the boardwalk searching for a place to drop his pants. Finally, he saw what looked like a log and decided that this would be a perfect spot. After relieving himself, he looked about for a scrap of paper, and seeing a white object in the sand next to him, he reached for it. Pulling on it, he noticed that it was a handkerchief, and on the second pull, found that a hand was holding on to the other end. He became so rattled that he pulled up his pants and started to run. Forgetting to duck, he hit his head against one of the planks under the boardwalk and was knocked cold. And that is how we found him, lying on his stomach, his behind covered with sand and dung, and a lump on his head as big as a tennis ball.

We dragged Shemp out and into the water to clean him up. He later explained that what he thought was a log was really a pair of young lovers lying in the sand. Although the situation was very funny, it ruined our night with the girls.

At age sixteen, between playing vaudeville and playing hooky, I had the opportunity to buy my first car, an old auto of uncertain vintage. The price: ninety dollars. I had only fifty to my name.

This monstrous hulk of a car had a right-hand drive with four progressive speeds mounted on the outside within reach of the driver, a long-handled brake alongside the gearshift, headlights powered by an acetylene tank, a convertible top for a sporty look, and a large bulb horn—the last word in accessories. It was the longest car I had ever seen and *everything* was in perfect working order . . . well almost everything. The brakes left a lot to be desired.

This car of my dreams was called a Pope Hartford. The company made one other model: the Pope Toledo. My only problem was how to buy a ninety-dollar car with just fifty dollars. I found the solution when I showed the car to Shemp.

"If you put up forty dollars, Shemp," I said, "you can buy a half ownership in it and I'll teach you how to drive."

Thirty minutes later, Shemp and I were the proud co-owners of a Pope Hartford with no linings on the brake drums. This problem was soon solved, too. If I wanted to stop the car I would apply the brake pedal about four hundred feet from my destination.

The car had what they called a cut-out, which made a terrible racket, and the folks in the neighborhood asked us not to drive past their homes or the church on Sunday before 10:30 A.M.

It was a Sunday morning—after 10:30—when Shemp asked me when he would get his first driving lesson. I said, "Right now." I came to a stop, no easy task, and let Shemp slide into the driver's seat. I showed him how to put the car in gear, feed it some spark and gas, and pull away from the curb. We then proceeded to motor along uneventfully, until we came to a quiet little business street. Suddenly Shemp spotted a little girl on roller skates about a block away, and screamed, "Moe, what do I do?"

I told him I would let him know when to apply the brakes and when to blow the horn. Shemp kept yelling, "Now, Moe, now?"

I said, "Okay, put on the brakes." He jammed down on them and slowed up some. Then I instructed, "Shemp, blow the horn." With that he let go of the wheel to squeeze the bulb horn with both hands. Before a sound came from the horn, the car went through the front window of a barber shop and stopped when it hit the barber chair. Shemp almost passed out. Fortunately the shop was closed on Sunday. The car was hauled out of the shop and deposited in our backyard, and our family was out thirty-two dollars for the window, four dollars for repairing the bootblack stand we ran over, and six dollars for the tow. It took us about three years to pay our dad back. Shemp never drove a car from that day until the day he died in 1955. In many of our films when Shemp was supposed to be driving a car, it actually was being pulled along by one of the prop men.

For two months, our car sat in the backyard. We finally found someone who seemed interested in purchasing it for eighty dollars, and we told him to bring the money and take the car. The next day, he inspected his purchase: he lifted the hood, looked in and said, "Just a minute, there's something missing—like the spark plugs, the carburator, the generator . . ."

Shemp yelled, "Somebody picked it clean!" So we sold it to him—as is—for twenty dollars. When he left, I said to Shemp, "This deal cost us seventy dollars plus another forty-two for the accident. We'll give Dad the twenty, right?"

"Right Moe! But the next time you call me into a business deal, I'm letting you know now—nothing doing!"

The Showboat "Sunflower"

WHEN I WAS A TEENAGER, everyone interested in fairs, circuses, Broadway theater, vaudeville, and the stock companies read *Billboard* magazine. It was my own favorite trade paper; I read everything about show business, but I was especially interested in the stock companies, and I'd follow every detail about them: where the companies were playing, the names of the plays, their casts. It was fascinating reading about the plays I had watched from the galleries of the Grand Opera House, the Crescent Theater, and the Montauk Theater (all in Brooklyn). What really intrigued me in *Billboard* were the want ads for the stock companies: Wanted, leading man, medium height—5'8"-5'11"; middle-aged man to play character parts; young soubrette to play both young and old. All the ads specified that the actors supply their own wardrobe—even army costumes. Another might ask for female leads who could also sing and dance. Every week I would pore through the news and ads. The names of the plays always intrigued me: *Ten Nights in a Barroom, The Two Orphans, The Misleading Lady, Nellie, the Sewing Machine Girl, Seven Keys to Baldpate, Uncle Tom's Cabin.*

There was also the *Circle Stock Company* which consisted of six independent stock companies in six different cities. A company would start in Akron, Ohio, and then go to Youngstown while a second would open in Akron. Then the first company would go on to Dayton, Columbus, Angola, Indiana, and Terre Haute, and then start over again with a new play.

Late in May 1914 I bought a *Billboard.* In it was an ad that altered my life, and put me into the kind of show business I loved most:

> *WANTED!* Young man—average height—to play juvenile parts and do general business parts. Must have own wardrobe. Send photo. If necessary can send fare. Capt. Billy Bryant, *The Showboat, Sunflower*—Dock side 8, Jackson, Mississippi.

I read the ad again and again. How could I apply? Would I have a chance of getting the job? I wasn't quite eighteen, I was rather short (5' 4") and weighed 120 soaking wet. I had no wardrobe. How could I overcome so many handicaps? It puzzled me for days. The best I could do for a wardrobe was a long suit from my brother Jack, but the photograph had me really stumped. If I could only present myself in person to Captain Bryant, he'd see my potential. Where would I get the money, though, for the railroad fare to Jackson, Mississippi? Then, I happened to glance up at a tinted photograph on the wall above my bed. It was a picture of Arthur Bramdon, a neighbor. He was good looking, medium height, with dark brown hair. He was a photographic model for the stereopticon slides that were between films in movie theaters.

As I stared at Arthur's photograph, an idea came to me: I'd mail Arthur's picture to Captain Bryant!

The next day I made the mistake of telling Shemp about my idea. He said I was out of my mind. "You'll wind up on a Mississippi chain gang for the rest of your life. . . . Mama will have a heart attack." I listened but paid no attention. This was my great opportunity and I could think of nothing else. I had to hurry before someone else answered the ad. I wrote a short note, didn't mention anything about my age, weight, or height, and enclosed the photo. I figured the handsome face of Arthur Bramdon would allay any doubts in Captain Bryant's mind.

Shemp and I were becoming very chummy at this time, and he had started inviting me to parties with him. I was surprised to find that he was becoming a good comedy entertainer and was playing the ukulele like a pro. He told me of a fellow who would write a vaudeville act for us in which we would do blackface. I told him I would think it over. He seemed elated that I was even considering the offer, although I did not let on that I had answered Captain Bryant's ad.

In the meantime, Shemp's friend had finished writing the blackface routine for us. I just couldn't get enthused over the material, though. Not long afterward, our mailbox was stuffed with a large envelope from Jackson, Mississippi—the thickest envelope I'd ever seen. It must have weighed over a pound. I ran up to my room and closed the door. Afraid of being disappointed, I put the package in my drawer under some clothes and went out for another breath of air. I was choking with excitement. I had to tell Shemp about it, although I knew he'd be upset that his vaudeville plans might go down the drain.

That night I asked Shemp to sit on my bed with me. I opened my drawer and showed him the still-unopened envelope. I told him what I thought might be in it and that I would probably have to put off doing an act with him until some later date, that he should get someone else to take my place. Shemp turned white and my heart pounded like a hammer. I carefully opened the package. There it was! A railroad mileage book loaded with little perforated coupons. In those days, if you took a train for any distance, they didn't issue single tickets to your destination, but rather little mileage books. If you went to a point three hundred miles away the conductor would tear out coupons that totaled up to three hundred miles. This enabled one to get on and off the train in different cities.

Also enclosed was a note telling me I was expected in Jackson as soon as possible. There was a wish for a pleasant journey and a signature: Captain Billy Bryant.

"You're mad!" cried Shemp. "Those tickets must cost at least seventy-five dollars. For Christ's sake, I can see you breaking rocks on a chain gang in that malaria-ridden country. What will happen to Mama and Papa? What will happen to me and our vaudeville act? You're insane and should be put away." Then, crying, he put his arm around my shoulder. "I wish to God I had your nerve and I wish you luck. If you get into trouble, write me and I'll do whatever I can. I'll tell Mama and Papa that you got a job in Philadelphia and will write at the first opportunity."

With a borrowed ten dollars, I left my Brooklyn home on March 12, 1914. The long, fourteen-hour train ride was transformed into a play in my mind in which I was acting the parts of all those magnificent performers that I loved as a boy. In no time, it seemed, the conductor was calling, "Jackson . . . Jackson, Mississippi." I grabbed my little bag and raincoat and jumped off the train as it was beginning to pull out of the station. Then came my first taste of fear. Would Captain Bryant accept me or throw me in jail? Was it too late to run away from this terrible situation I had created? I decided that I had come so far that there was no turning back. Besides, what man would jail me for only trying to achieve a goal? True, I had lied and cheated, a little. But I was just trying to do the thing I loved—to be an actor. Who could hate me for that? Questions and answers raced through my head.

The next morning was St. Patrick's Day and that gave me a feeling of good luck and confidence as I boarded the showboat *Sunflower.* I pushed the button on Captain Bryant's doorjamb. A loud voice bellowed, "Come in!" Beads of perspiration gathered on my forehead. "Come in!" the captain shouted. It sounded like the voice of doom; to me, it was the moment of truth. I had regained full control of myself by the time I opened the door and stood facing Captain Bryant. He stared at me long and hard. I was searching for some part of a smile but there was none. "What can I do for you?" he asked. Soon the twinkle in his eye faded as I mustered up my nerve to start my pitch: "Captain, did you receive the picture I sent you?" He looked down at his desk. My eyes followed as he looked at the photo of Arthur, then at me, and back to the picture.

"No! My God, no! It can't be. Oh, no! How could anyone pull a stunt like this?" Captain Bryant extended his forefinger nearly touching my face. He growled, "Do you know what I can do to you for this? How could you believe you could get away with this?" After his initial explosion, I broke in, pleadingly, "You wouldn't gain a thing if you put me in jail. Putting me to work—even on a menial job—would benefit you in the long run and you'd also know that you were instrumental in helping me toward my goal."

I watched every expression, looking for a sign, listening for those words that would mean my future. The captain spoke hesitantly. "Boy, you've got yourself a job . . . doing something or other. You'll get your room and board and twenty dollars a week which will be deducted from your debt—for the railroad ticket and the ad I will have to put in *Billboard* to get the man I've been looking for. You'll mop the auditorium and clean it up each day, and the dressing rooms twice a week at night. You'll give out the programs and usher the people to their seats. When you've paid your debt there will be an additional thirty-two dollars for your fare home. But if I decide to keep you on for the rest of the summer, I will continue to pay you twenty dollars each week." I thanked him profusely. "You know, Captain Bryant, I'm going to be an actor—a very good one!" He finally smiled. "With your ungodly nerve, I believe you can be anything."

The season opened on April 8, 1914, with *The Bells,* starring Thomas E. Shea. I had seen this play before at the Grand Opera House in Brooklyn but never cared for it; it was too melodramatic. The second week's play, also one I knew, was *Human Hearts.* I asked Captain Bryant if he'd let me do the part of the half-wit boy. I felt it was made to order for me. I was surprised when he allowed me to read the role at rehearsal.

After my reading, the captain said, "Harry,* you've got the part of Sam. See what you can do with it. I'll be watching you and if you're as good an actor as you are a liar, I'll be satisfied." This was my first professional stage appearance. The fact that I had followed the character of Sam all through the play when I saw it from the gallery of the Crescent Theater back in Brooklyn helped me immeasurably. Captain Bryant was delighted and offered me a role in the next play, *Ten Nights in a Barroom*—Young Slade, the son of the bartender who kills his father with a whiskey bottle while in a drunken stupor. Again I played the part to the hilt and convinced everyone with my performance as a drunk.

Over the next few months, Captain Bryant raised my salary to thirty dollars a week. "You've already paid your debt and are well on your way to becoming an excellent actor. I'd recommend you highly to anyone." I told him I would like to stay on for at least two seasons. "Harry, you have a deal."

For two seasons on the *Sunflower,* I got to play most of the parts I had seen in the theaters as a boy. The season usually ran from May 12 until about September 10. By the end of my first season my salary was $65 a week; $100 a week in the second season.

It was a joyous experience. I had launched my career on the *Sunflower.* There I was, doing what I loved best, making a good living and helping support my family at the same time.

---

*Although my given name was Harry Moses Horwitz, in school I was known as Moe; in the early days of the theater, Harry; and then with Ted Healy, I again was Moe.

Breaking into Vaudeville with Shemp

AFTER A COUPLE OF SUMMERS with Captain Bryant on the *Sunflower,* I began my act with Shemp. I can recall our efforts to get started in show business, going from agent to agent. After weeks of doing the rounds, we felt pretty dejected. I had two seasons on the showboat under my belt and I'd done many films at Vitagraph Studio, and yet it was so tough to break into vaudeville. Shemp was extremely discouraged. I begged him to hold on for another week or so and if nothing came up by then, we would try films again. Two days later, we found an agent: a jovial black man with the two-bit Sheedy Agency. He asked me many questions regarding my show business background. I answered his questions, I ran down my own credits, and I did some important lying about Shemp. We told him that our stage name was Howard and Howard, which sounded better than Horwitz and Horwitz, and were hired for thirty dollars for three days—for the two of us. Mr. Sheedy gave us a contract for the Mystic Theater on 53rd Street near Third Avenue.

We would open on the following Friday and close on Sunday, doing a blackface act with about twelve minutes of comedy. The day before the opening we went to see the theater. It held approximately three hundred and the audience entered through an alley. The contract failed to mention how many shows we were to do, but it didn't matter to us; Shemp and I were in vaudeville.

It was midwinter—and bitter cold. The first show was eleven in the morning, but we arrived at the theater at nine and introduced ourselves to the manager, who directed us to our dressing room in the basement. Fortunately it adjoined the furnace which kept us from freezing to death. We put on our black makeup and sat with our feet up on the furnace, waiting to be called.

We were the comedy relief—last on the bill of four acts. When it was our turn, the manager would yell down to us, "Howard and Howard—up and at 'em." The sign would go up on the side of the proscenium, "Howard and Howard—A Study in Black," and we shuffled onto the stage to the tune of "Darktown Strutters' Ball." One fellow clapped on our entrance and that was the extent of our applause. The dialogue of the act (as best I can remember it) was as follows:

> MOE: All they do is give you beans. Beans for breakfast, beans for lunch, and
> beans for dinner. Why they even send you to war with a bean shooter.

There was no audience reaction, so we slid into some material that we had stolen from a well-known act of the day, *Moss and Frye*:

In style — as befitting
a rising young actor.

MOE: You think you're pretty smart spouting those big words at Mrs. Lincoln's party.
SHEMP: Yes, I am smart.
MOE: Okay, boy, what size is a gray suit? . . . Do you think it's as warm in the summer as it is in the country? . . . If you went to the railroad station and bought a ticket for three dollars, where are you going? And by the way, if three dimes is thirty cents, how much is a bunch of nickels?
SHEMP: Enough of that smart-aleck stuff, let's sing a song that will put our friends in a good humor.

At this point some people entered the theater from the alley door at the back of the stage, and with them a gust of wind and a bit of snow. The curtain, like a sail in the wind, pushed against our backs and nearly knocked us off the stage. We finished the song we were singing to a burst of silence, took three bows to the audience's back as they were leaving. To make a very long and horrible nightmare longer, we did six shows on Friday, nine shows on Saturday, and eight on Sunday. We realized finally that we were the "clean-up" act. Every time the theater filled up the manager would yell down, "Howard and Howard, up and at 'em!" Whenever he wanted to clear everyone out, up and at 'em we'd go, and the audience would leave the minute we came on. It was a heartbreaking experience but it never fazed us, for I knew we were getting better, our material was better, theater conditions were better—but the salary was the same.

Our blackface act was broken up briefly by World War I. Shemp was drafted into the army and went off to war. If they'd put him in the navy they might not have noticed that he was a bedwetter. He was discharged after a few months and came back to join me in vaudeville.

In 1916, my parents exchanged some property in Bensonhurst for a 116-acre farm in Chatham, New York, 150 miles from New York City and 60 miles from Springfield, Massachusetts.

28

I'd help on the farm with the planting in the spring and the harvesting in the fall. In between I'd work in vaudeville with Shemp. Our older brother, Jack, and a professional farmer worked on the farm full-time.

The farm had fourteen cows, two Percheron horses, and their two-year-old offspring, Nancy. In addition there was a sorrel horse and a thirteen-year-old "cribber" called John who would cause me no end of embarrassment by stopping in the busiest part of the street to leave his droppings. A "cribber" is a horse who grinds his teeth on fences or any other hard objects and constantly sucks air, causing him to make the weirdest noises. On several occasions, I left him hitched to a wagon to find him sound asleep on the shafts.

With the farm came a large, fat pig. My mother lost little time in throwing it off the farm, since pork did not at all fit into her Jewish lifestyle. The pig was sold and thirteen days later gave birth to a large litter of piglets.

Among the many Rhode Island reds and Plymouth Rocks was a multicolored hen we called Henrietta. She followed me everywhere. At milking time I got a kick out of spraying her with milk. One day Henry, as I named her, fell into a mound of cow manure. I rushed for my water bucket, washed her off, dried her with a burlap bag and then put her in a warm oven to dry. We almost had roast Henry when my brother Jack turned up the oven to cook something. I found her in the nick of time.

I can remember that whenever I would feed the chickens, Henry would perch on my shoulder, and as I would scatter corn to the other chickens, I'd cup my hand and feed Henry. One day, just as I stepped out of the barn, a hen hawk grabbed Henry and started to fly away with her. I picked up a rock and let the hawk have it. Henry dropped with a thud. She lived, but minus a few feathers. Finally a rather large horse trod on Henry, causing her demise at the age of four and a half months.

That summer, Curly, who was thirteen, joined us on the farm.

He pitched in with the chores and was anxious to learn to do everything, from running the cream separator to churning butter to helping cultivate the truck garden. He could handle the horses quite well and fed the livestock at 4:30 every morning while Shemp and I were milking the cows. Shemp didn't care much for farm work. He'd much rather play cowboy—without a horse—

With a fellow vaudevillian . . . high spirits in Springfield, Missouri.

Moe on tour in 1923.

in an unfenced field of corn. With a whip in his hand and an alarm clock tied to his belt, he'd let the cows feed in the pasture for a couple of hours and then would drive them back into the corral. Shemp's outfit for these farm chores: a pair of red flannels, a Continental Army coat, and a cocked hat. Every time a neighbor would drive by in his horse and buggy, Shemp would strike a pose in the middle of the field. Often neighbors would stop by and comment on that fantastic scarecrow in the cornfield.

One day Curly decided he wanted to do some mowing, so I put him on the machine and headed for the field of hay, and then walked along beside to see that he handled the mower properly. Curly was mowing for about an hour when he suddenly cut through a nest of yellow jackets. He jumped off the mower and we both raced for the nearby stream, followed closely by a swarm. Our necks and hands were covered with stings. It was days before the swellings went down.

We were always doing things just for laughs. I remember one time shaving only the right side of my face, and Shemp shaved the left side of his. When our half beards were really full and bushy, we went into town to watch the good folks hurriedly cross to the other side of the street. Then there was the time our mother sent us a wire that she was coming to Chatham for the weekend to look over the farm. Shemp and I dressed for her arrival: our red flannels, our Continental Army coats, our cocked hats. And our half beards gave us an added touch of insanity. We hitched up the team to our surrey with the fringe on top and drove into town to meet the train. Curly went along for the ride, for a little additional class, and warned us that Mother might be rather embarrassed seeing us look as we did, but we had too much of the theater in us to change our minds. We pulled the surrey up close to the station platform, and when the train came to a stop, Shemp and I were standing by, each holding a horse by the bridle.

Mother looked around for a few minutes and never recognized us. Then she saw Curly sitting in the surrey and, as she approached it, Shemp and I each took an arm and kissed her on each cheek. Mother, a very staid person, became terribly embarrassed because of the crowd that had gathered, and, as we drove away, asked us, "How can you do such crazy things? The people will think you're meshuga!"

Several days later Curly decided to go hunting with a neighbor. He took my rifle, a .22-caliber gun with a hair trigger. Curly later told us that he was sitting on the ground with his legs crossed and the end of the rifle barrel pointed at his foot. Without any thought that he had a rifle in his hand, he kept playing with the trigger. It discharged with a roar, sending the bullet into his ankle. He went up to our bedroom and there he lay, white as a sheet, blood oozing from his foot. We had him rushed to St. Peter's Hospital in Albany, sixty miles away, where it was touch and go as to whether he would lose his foot.

I dread to think what would have happened if our mother had been there at the time.

For six days, I walked the three and a half miles from our farm to the railroad station in Chatham, took the train to Albany to visit with Curly for a couple of hours, and talked to the doctors about him. They told me that in about six months his instep and ankle bones should be broken and put in a cast so that he would be able to bend his ankle. Curly decided against this and, although it gave him much pain and he limped his way through life, he never let it interfere with his work . . . or for that matter his play.

In 1917 Shemp and I worked our comedy act for both the Loew's and RKO circuits. This was

With two handsome shepherds,
while touring in Alabama.

unheard of, as there was an unwritten agreement between the two circuits. If you worked for one, the other wouldn't hire you. We got around this by playing a blackface act for RKO and a whiteface act for Loew's.

The theaters, at the time, held between two hundred and four hundred people, but the owners weren't very dependable, so we had to make certain that we'd get the $12.50 for our two days work. To solve our problem we found an agent who would be responsible for collecting our salary. One act that we worked with was a contortionist, Ferry the Frogman, who was breaking in a new act at the time. During one part of his routine he would fold his legs behind his neck and sit on a very small whiskey glass. Every night he would take about twenty minutes to limber up. His costumes were an integral part of the act. For the matinee, Ferry would wear a green frog costume made of thousands of sparkling white sequins; for his evening performance he wore a smashing suit with the opposite colors.

I remember one night we all went to dinner. I ordered a sardine sandwich, Shemp a ham and cheese, and Ferry ordered a double burger and beans. After dinner we returned to the theater. Shemp and I finished our act, then Ferry came on stage in his beautiful white suit covered with green sequins. He made a frog-like entrance walking on his hands, and after twisting himself into some unbelievable positions, he placed a small whiskey glass on the stage and proceeded to lock his legs behind his neck. After staying in that position about two minutes, he started to turn as green as his costume, then vomited all over his elegant attire. It was then that the stage hands noticed that he was stuck in that pretzel shape and was unable to untangle himself. They ran on stage, lifted him up, tangles and all, and carried him off.

The next day he was well enough to do the two shows. He explained that usually he had only a glass of milk for supper and ate his dinner after the last performance. Hamburger and beans, he later told us, were just too much for his pretzel-shaped colon. The next day he sent his costume to the cleaners. The cleaning cost more than the salary he had earned.

At the Peerless in Brooklyn, Shemp and I appeared on the bill with an acrobatic act, "Page, Hack, and Mack." Page, a contortionist, was Mack's wife. Mack was a behemoth of a man, six feet tall and 240 pounds; Hack, a short, stocky German, weighed only 124 and was five foot seven.

The act's only prop was a table without a top. Hack would stand in the opening of the table and, as the music played and the drums rolled, he'd leap straight into the air and land with his feet on the edges of the table frame. Then, as Hack jumped in the air again, the frame of the table was slid into place. More frames and tops were added until Hack was standing on top of six tables, each 30 inches high. At this point, Page wrapped herself around Mack's stomach, holding her ankles with her hands. Now as the music rose to a crescendo, Mack would step up to the footlights with Page wrapped around his middle; he would be facing the audience. Mack would raise his muscular arms into the air, and as the drum roll increased, Hack would leap forward off the tables with arms extended and Mack would catch him with a hand-to-hand grip, just stopping him from flying off the stage and into the orchestra pit. It was a breathtaking trick.

The act went well for the first two days, but on the second show of the closing day, Hack leaped, his hands hit Mack's hands, and he slid right through, plummeting head first into the orchestra pit. There were screams from the audience and then a hush as Hack got to his feet, bowed slowly, acknowledging their wild applause, and then passed out.

Hack was taken to the hospital where he was thought to have a fractured skull. Later he explained that he had forgotten to wipe the rosin bag over his hands to keep them from slipping.

This was vaudeville, and Shemp and I continued with this insanity until 1922.

Helen

Moe and his wife, Helen (1927).

I MET MY WIFE HELEN on the beach in Bensonhurst in 1922. Here was this charming young lady with fantastic legs, dressed in an old-fashioned bathing suit, all covered up—even long silk stockings. As she emerged from the water, I noticed her stockings were in shreds and dye from her suit was running down her legs.

After a letter-writing courtship for three years, I married Helen Schonberger (she was a cousin of Harry Houdini) in Brooklyn. I had been touring in vaudeville for weeks at a time, so I used letters and poems to keep our relationship alive. She kept all the old poems hidden away for all these years.

Our wedding day was quite trying for me. I was talked into wearing tails and a high hat by relatives of the bride-to-be. Before I left for the ceremony, I peeked out of a crack in the door to make sure none of my friends would see me in this wardrobe. Finally, high hat in hand, I ran out of the door into a cab that was at the corner about a hundred yards away. I'm sure I did that hundred in no time flat. I expected to be pelted with tomatoes and other soft vegetables. I guess I remembered what I'd done to high hats in my youth, but I made it.

Helen looked beautiful as a bride and to this day still looks beautiful despite nearly fifty years of marriage to a Stooge. No gold pie plates, please!

Shemp married Gertrude Frank that same year. She was the daughter of a builder who lived in the Bensonhurst area. Gertrude was nicknamed Babe, and I guess that was why we took to calling our Babe Curly. It had gotten very confusing.

Joining Forces with Ted Healy

IN THE WINTER OF 1922, I spotted a newspaper ad announcing that Ted and Betty Healy were appearing on an eight-act vaudeville bill at Brooklyn's Prospect Theater. I had not seen Ted in ten years.

It was bitter cold and snowing the day I got to the stage door of the Prospect and came face to face with Ted. We hugged each other and Ted said, "The good Lord must have sent you."

I replied, "An ad in the paper sent me." He had grown a good twelve inches since 1912, making him more than six feet tall. He was about twenty-five; I was nine months younger and eight inches shorter. I learned that things had not gone well for him in business, and it had taken him ten years to realize that he really wasn't cut out to be a businessman. He finally tried the theater, and it was then that he changed his name to Ted Healy and improved his financial status.

After we reminisced for a while, he worked his way around to feeling me out about joining forces with him in a new act he wanted to test. "I make a speech to the audience and then proceed to pour water on the acrobat who is lying down in a box," he said. "I'd call it Fire and Water. You jump out and do a back flip like you used to do at the beach." I reminded him that the stage was wood with cement beneath it. The beach was soft sand. He explained that he would have the dancer and another guy hold me up with a rope. Well, I tried the stunt and as my legs came over from the back flip I kicked one of the men in the neck and the other in the chin. Both of them quit.

An idea for a new sight gag struck me. I would jump straight up and grab Ted by the waistband of his pants. I tried it and pulled Ted's pants clear off.

Ted was elated. "That's it," he said. "We'll do it that way for more laughs." Ted explained that he did his regular act with his wife Betty and their dog Pete and also owned a dancing act, doing two turns on the bill and getting nine hundred and fifty dollars for both. The next day several bookers and Ted's agent were coming to the matinee to catch his act. First he would do his routine with Betty and Pete, then clown around in the dancing act, asking for a young man to volunteer assistance. I was to jump on the stage and hand him a note, then do the bit with him. It worked so well that he asked me to hang around a few days until he could get an acrobat. The two days lasted nine years. When we closed at the end of the first week, Ted had new contracts for five weeks on the Delmar circuit in the South and another five on the Interstate circuit in Texas.

The act was a smash; before long Healy was getting $3,500 a week. He was giving me one hundred dollars a week.

It was 1925. I was just making my stage entrance at the Orpheum in Brooklyn when I heard an unmistakable laugh coming from the audience. It was my brother Shemp. I turned to Ted and whispered that Shemp was somewhere out there. Ted walked to the footlights, peered into the darkened theater, and said, "I would like to have another young man come up, preferably one from Brooklyn." Up came Shemp, munching on a pear, a pair of rubbers in his pocket—he always carried rubbers in case of rain. Grace Hayes was on the bill that day with her ten-year-old son, Peter Lind. One of the songs in their act was "Dirty Hands, Dirty Face." When Ted saw Shemp coming, he had the orchestra play Grace's music. Enjoying the whole thing, Shemp asked Ted if he'd like a bite of his pear. Ted refused, Shemp tried to force it on him, Ted smashed it over Shemp's face, and the battle was on. This routine was to become part of the act—along with Shemp.

A short time later, while we were waiting to open in a theater in Chicago, we decided to catch the stage show at the Marigold Gardens. Along with the usual singers and comedians, there was a young blond fellow in high silk hat and tails, playing the violin and doing a Russian dance. The effect was one of incongruity. I looked at Ted and asked, "Are you thinking what I'm thinking?" and he said, "Yes, I'm thinking what you're thinking!" At the end of the show, we went back stage to talk to this odd-looking character. He was wearing a robe and his hair, which was wet after a shower, was drying in the wildest manner. Ted invited him to join our act, offering him ninety dollars a week—ten dollars more if he'd get rid of the violin. He accepted, and Larry Fine became the third Stooge in 1925. The act became Ted Healy and His Three Southern Gentlemen.

Larry Fine had been Fineberg back in South Philadelphia—at least that's the story I got from him. He had begun violin lessons almost before learning to walk. To help strengthen his arm muscles after a bad acid burn as an infant, his parents had started him on the classical violin. Larry had been a very slight child, and, in his late teens, he weighed less than 115 pounds. A lightweight, he did quite well as an amateur boxer. This must have given him the strength to take all the punishment that I dished out through the years. He realized quite early that classical music wasn't for him, so he decided to give popular music a go, and started his show business career before becoming a teenager, doing a comedy singing routine in Jewish dialect. He auditioned his act for Gus Edwards's brother, Ben, and got a spot in Ben's version of the Newsboy Sextet (the original starred Billy Gould, Herman Timberg, Georgie Price, George Jessel, Walter Winchell, and Eddie Cantor). He stayed with the group for a short time, got homesick, and quit.

When World War I broke out, he put together an act with a girl named Nancy Decker and played army camps and hospitals around the United States. Shortly afterwards, he did a vaudeville dance act with the Haney Sisters, Loretta and Mabel, and married Mabel in 1927. In the years before they were married, though, Mabel had "stolen" Nancy Decker from Larry and made her one of the Haney Sisters. Undeterred, Larry found himself a new partner, Winona Fine. They couldn't bring themselves to calling the act Fine and Fine, so they settled for Fine and Dandy—which didn't work out too well either.

For the next few years, Larry played violin with Howard Lanin's Orchestra at the Roseland Dance Hall in Philadelphia and entered Amateur Night shows, playing a makeshift violin (part cigar box, part broom handle with strings attached; it was played like a cello). Then his brother-in-law, agent Harry Romm (later the Stooges' agent and a Columbia Pictures executive), got him a spot with Mel Klee, the blackface comedian. At this point, Larry joined the Haney Sisters again and with them played theaters throughout the Midwest. At the end of their tour, the Haney Sisters and Fine split up, and Larry was again doing a single as a blackface comedian. He opened at the Paramount Theater in Toronto. Not long afterward, Larry decided to join a theatrical club, figuring that it might help him meet producers and agents. He played cards with producer Leroy Prinz and nightclub owner Fred Mann, who ran the Rainbow Gardens. One night, Ray Evans, who was emceeing at Mann's club, quit in a billing dispute (Ruth Etting was the star of the show). Larry, who was at the right place at the right time—the card table with Mann and Prinz—was offered a tryout. Mann and Prinz were impressed and Larry was given a seven-year contract to play Mann's Chicago club and the Jai Alai Fronton in Havana.

When Ted made Larry the offer to join our act backstage at the Rainbow Gardens, one problem remained: Larry's contract with Mann. A few nights later, fate stepped in when the police closed the Rainbow Gardens for violation of the Prohibition laws. Not only was the Garden shut down, but Fred Mann committed suicide. There now was no contract problem and Larry was in the act.

Ted Healy and His Three Southern Gentlemen did vaudeville all through 1926 into 1927, when Shemp left to do a Broadway revue, *A Night in Spain,* with Ted and Betty Healy, Phil Baker, Grace Hayes, Georgie Price, Sid Silvers, Helen Kane, and others. I remember how the *New York Times* spoke of Shemp in its review: "He whom the program describes as Shemp Howard made the most of an exceedingly comic face and a diffident manner."

Ted, Shemp, Larry, and I went back into vaudeville in 1928 with a new act, Ted Healy and the Racketeers, complete with a rigged cyclorama curtain, cut in three breakaway sections. The routine we did went this way: the curtain opened with Ted hanging on a trapeze and Shemp and I standing beside a twelve-foot ladder just under Ted's feet. As he started to make a speech, Shemp and I would jerk the ladder out from under him. "Hey, fellows, bring back the ladder." We'd put it under his feet again and he would start once more: "Ladies and gentlemen, I am now going to do a little chinning." We again would pull the ladder away while he tried to chin himself, and not being able to make it, he'd start yelling, "Moe, Shemp, get the ladder!" We'd rush towards him but since the ladder was so unwieldy, we'd run right past him into the back curtain. A stagehand would then pull the sash line and the whole back curtain would fall, exposing a young couple kissing. Ted kept screaming, "The ladder! Get the ladder!" Again we would stagger toward him—and into the other side curtain. Down the left curtain would crash with Ted still yelling. Then we'd stagger to the right and that curtain would fall. Ted would still be screaming as the stage curtain came down, "Get the ladder!" Our going-off music would continue and another act went on for about twelve minutes. Then the curtain would open again and Ted was still hanging on the trapeze yelling for the ladder. Finally we got the ladder under his feet, he'd come down, give us a double slap, and we'd bow to ringing applause.

Passover week of 1927 was particularly tough for the act. We were doubling between the Orpheum and the Bushwick theaters in Brooklyn when Ted got us an unexpected booking at the Hippodrome Theater in New York that weekend, filling in for Cantor Rosenblatt, who was singing there that week but would not work on Passover. Luckily, there were only two performances a day in these topflight theaters. On Monday we went from the Orpheum to the Bushwick. We had breakaway scenery and both theaters were rigged for the breakaway curtains—all we had to do was to put the curtains in one cab and the four of us would follow in another. We were third on an eight-act bill in the Orpheum and seventh on the bill at the Bushwick; it was the same schedule matinees and evenings.

On Wednesday, Shemp and I promised our mother that we would have the Passover seder at her place, so Ted, Shemp, and I took a cab to my parents' home in Bensonhurst. Dad purposely rushed the services so we could get back on time for our night show.

During the seder, Shemp proceeded to get high on wine. Embarrassed for my mother and annoyed with Shemp, Ted said, "You know, mom, that Shemp is an *imbecile*." Whereupon my mother replied indignantly, "What's the matter with my Moe?" It seems that she thought that Ted was paying Shemp a compliment and since she never wished to show any partiality to any of her five sons, she wanted me to participate in the compliment. Now came Friday night and the eight fifteen show at the Hippodrome and the matinee on Saturday in addition to the two shows at the Orpheum and the Bushwick. What a rat race! It took us three weeks to recuperate from that one week. Ted received $1,500 for the Hippodrome date and $3,000 each for the other two dates. We got our standard $100 each.

We did vaudeville all over the South and Midwest and even got a bigtime nightclub date on the outskirts of Chicago. In one place we were hired for a very swanky society dinner. We hired a piano player, put on rented tuxedos, and found ourselves at a posh dinner of the Black and White Society, so named because the men wore starched black dress shirts, white tuxedos, and white bow ties; the women wore white dresses with black scarfs around their necks. They really looked grotesque. For high society, I never saw so much drinking in my life, or heard so many off-color jokes. The woman who booked us had been concerned whether our slapstick-style routines would be offensive. She followed us around like a mother hen. When Larry started talking to one of the women guests, she whispered in his ear, "You performers are not to mingle with the guests." Larry turned to go just as one of the Black and White women vomited all over him.

After cleaning him up and paying one of the busboys five dollars for the loan of his jacket, we went on. Following a short fanfare our piano player introduced us as Ted Healy and His Gang. We started to go into our act when one of the charming young women threw a roll at us. More followed. Healy yelled, "Boys, let's hold out for the roast beef." It was a regular free-for-all. Finally Healy said, "Let's get out of this high-class jungle!"

Not long after our society episode, we were booked into a dinner for the Hay and Grain Association. We were to appear at seven and the dinner was to be at eight thirty. By seven the men were already feeling no pain and were whooping it up like wild men. Ted Healy and His Gang were introduced and I'm sure no one heard the introduction. To get their attention, the piano player tried a chorus of "When the Saints Go Marching In"; nothing helped. Suddenly, one guest yelled, "Let's get the funny man," and then with his spoon flipped a pat of butter at Ted. It missed him, but landed on my adam's apple. Then all hell broke loose, and butter pats were flying in every direction, and the men were laughing like hyenas. Healy screamed, "Cut the act," and we walked off. The agent handed Ted the check and apologized profusely. Ted asked her if she could possibly book us at quiet dinners.

Ted Healy and His Southern Gentlemen, Larry Fine
and Moe and Shemp Howard, in 1925.

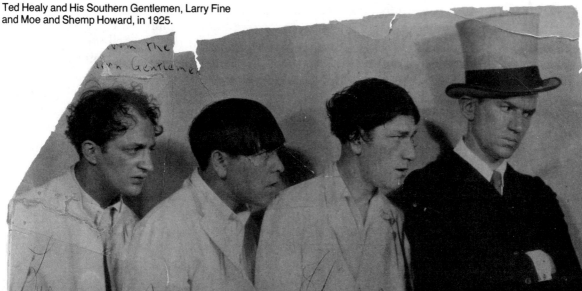

My Daughter
Is Born and
a Brief Leave
from Show
Business

Daddy Moe Howard with Joan (1928).

IN 1927, WHILE TED AND SHEMP were doing *A Night In Spain* on Broadway, Larry married Mabel Haney. It also was the year Helen gave birth to our daughter Joan.

At this time, we were living on Avenue J near Coney Island Avenue in Brooklyn. Helen had a rather easy pregnancy—the normal craving for strange foods and the kicking belly. The time of the delivery was when *we* had *our* difficulties. Helen's pains started one night, so off we went to the hospital. Once there, her labor was endless. I would come into her hospital room to give her some encouragement, I'd hear a moan or a groan and, softy that I am, I'd run like hell out of the room into the waiting area. There I took to counting the call chimes that would ring out intermittently—two short chimes, then a space, then three chimes and a pause, and then one chime. This kept on constantly until I found myself pointing my finger, like a fight referee, trying to predict the exact moment a chime would ring out. I was doing this for some time, improving all the while as the minutes wore on. Then I looked up and realized that the seven or eight people in the waiting room with me had started leaving, until I found myself sitting there alone. It finally dawned on me that they must have thought I was nuts.

The labor went on and on and on. After what seemed an eternity, they wheeled Helen into the delivery room. As they pushed her past me, I remember saying, "Honey, never again! Never again, I just can't take it." It took over eight years for us to forget our pains and try again.

Being on the road so much touring with Ted and the boys in vaudeville posed a problem which had to be worked out. At the time of my marriage to Helen two years before, her Aunt Fanny predicted that if she married an actor, she would never have a home. Ironically, several members of Helen's family were in show business, including Harry Houdini, the world-famous magician. It was too bad that Aunt Fanny did not live to see the happy future in store for Helen and Moe Horwitz and the elegant English manor house we built in Toluca Lake, California, across the street from Bing Crosby.

With these thoughts in mind, I let myself be prevailed upon to leave show business when Shemp went to Broadway with Ted. I went into real estate and was successful in buying some property at a very reasonable price. Then I proceeded to build a couple of one-family brick houses, using contractors who generally were old schoolmates of mine. When the buildings were completed, I realized that I had built them too well. They were just too expensive for the Brooklyn neighborhood and would not bring my price or anything near the cost of construction. The bank took over the properties and I was advised to file for bankruptcy. I felt I could not do this to all my friends, so I paid all of them except the brick man, who got his money from the bank when they sold the houses. I finally came out with $425 from an investment of $22,000. It was a shame that my folks were on a trip to Lithuania to visit their old hometown, for business-minded mother could have been a great help to me.

When everything was settled, I found myself with a couple of hundred dollars, an understanding wife, and a beautiful eight-month-old daughter. Actually, I was discouraged but tried not to show my concern when Helen was around.

Once again I was advised to go into business for myself, but what kind? All I was geared for was show business; I lived and breathed it. I was rated as a good dramatic actor and an excellent comic. Now a friend suggested that I open a shop and sell distressed merchandise, which I'd buy at auction. The deal sounded reasonable to me, so I rented a store for thirty dollars a month. My friend took me to various auctions and directed me when to buy and how much to pay. That day I invested all the money I had except four dollars. I bought umbrellas, ladies' pure silk hosiery, tea sets in cartons, white silk gloves, bloomers, small bottle of beads, house dresses, etc. This friend had a small truck in which we carted all my merchandise to the store. I was tired, upset, and scared; but I showed Helen a cheerful and confident Moe. I said, "Honey, it's only one o'clock. We'll have some lunch and I'll drive you and the baby to the shop. We'll separate the merchandise and put it out on display."

Anxious to show Helen my fantastic buys, I immediately untied the cord that held the four bundles of umbrellas, twenty-five in each bundle. As I opened the first umbrella, it fell into shreds as did all the others. Helen laughed until she became hysterical, but I was so depressed that the tears ran down my face. I thought my heart would break. What kind of mess did I get myself into this time? Helen tried to comfort me. I couldn't understand it; all the items they had shown me at the auction looked new. Now I opened the bundles of silk hosiery, and they too fell apart. The white silk gloves were so small they wouldn't fit a child and most of them were for the left hand. The tea sets, as were some of the other things, were burned and smoked. Helen kissed me and said, "We'll try to sell this junk, and if we can't and you still want to go back into the theater, you should do it."

Things really looked bleak. Some days we hardly took in enough money to buy food for ourselves. We lived in a lovely apartment and our furnishings were the finest. I was too proud to ask my parents for help. We decided to wait it out. The only things that were in good condition were the bloomers, made of a sort of lacy, mesh material. I remember being asked by a customer about this type of garment. Having no idea what they were, I told her, "they're coozy ventilators," whatever that meant. I sold all the coozy ventilators and made $62.50. I was now in the fifth week of that impossible dream. After settling with the landlord, Helen and I walked out of that store and we never mentioned it again. It was as though a weight had been lifted from my shoulders.

Back with Ted Healy

THAT NIGHT, after leaving the store and putting a business career behind me, I realized that my resources were almost nil. I had to find a job and decided to phone Ted Healy. I inquired about his health and his family's health and he told me, "You know, Moe, I was going to phone you in the morning to ask if you, Shemp, and Larry would join me in the Shuberts' *A Night in Venice* on Broadway. We go into rehearsal in three weeks and open the second week in January. How about it, Moe?" I was speechless.

Helen whispered, "Tell him that you'll let him know."

I felt like floating on air. My spirits had been at such a low point for a year and a half. I phoned Ted later at his home in Connecticut and told him that I'd join him. He said he'd send his chauffeur for Helen, Joan, and me in the morning, and we could stay at his home in Connecticut until rehearsal started.

Ted was a star now. He had a new foreign car, a Renault. His home in Darien, Connecticut, was palatial: twenty-six rooms, including twelve bedrooms with a fireplace in each. And the grounds were magnificent. There was a seemingly endless pine grove, covered with very valuable specimen trees and the usual babbling brook. It was a wonderful change for me and my family; we spent a Christmas there that I shall never forget.

Ted's wife and vaudeville partner at the time (who used to be half of a dancing act—the Braun Sisters) was the former Betty Braun. She made *us* feel very welcome, although there were some very uncomfortable moments between her and Ted.

I remember when Betty arrived in Darien she came in the front door as Ted rushed a showgirl he was having an affair with out the back door. I also remember how, during the week, a package arrived from J. J. Shubert with a dozen magnificent handkerchiefs for Betty and nothing for Ted. In a rage, he threw Betty's gift into the fireplace.

We had gotten to Ted's place in time for lunch and talked right through the night, developing material for the show, some of which we used to the end of our vaudeville days—material like the sketch where we enter on stage and Ted asks us, "Who are you gentlemen?"

"We're from the South."

"So you're from the South," Ted says. "Did you ever hear of Abraham Lincoln?" Whereupon I extend my hand to Ted and say, "Glad to meetcha, stranger."

At this point, for the first time, Ted gives us the triple slap, hitting, machine-gun-like, across our three faces.

In another sketch, Ted is in the cockpit of an airplane and, pointing to the gas gauge, says, "How much fuel do we have?" Shemp replies, "I don't know, Ted, I looked at the gauge and the arrow points half way. I don't know if it's half-empty or half-full." For this retort Ted gave Shemp a sharp rap over the head.

Another one had Ted saying to Larry, "Did you take a bath this morning?"

"No, somebody was in the bathroom," said Larry.

"What time was that?"

"About nine in the morning," said Larry.

"That was my wife," Ted replied.

"Ain't she skinny!"

A Night in Venice, which was staged by Busby Berkeley, played three weeks of break-in dates in New Haven, Atlantic City, and Akron, and then opened on Broadway in May 1929. I remember how critic Brooks Atkinson described Shemp, Larry, and me as "three of the frowziest numskulls ever assembled." The show went over very well and ran for seventeen weeks. Then we went on the road until 1929 when it closed because of the Depression.

While rehearsing for *A Night in Venice,* we were working with Ted Healy, along with the Stevens Brothers and their wrestling bear.

Healy came up with the bright idea of making our entrance on stage with a dozen or more cats following closely at our heels. But how to get a dozen cats and teach them the art of acting?

I told Ted I'd locate the cats, but he'd have to figure a way of training them. "Okay," Ted said, "Go get the cats and we'll keep them in the men's room." We were rehearsing on the second floor of the Sardi Building on 44th Street. My plan was to stand out in front of a little movie theater on Eighth Avenue and when some kids came out, I'd give each fifty cents to bring me a good-size cat. I went back to the rehearsal room and waited. Soon, one kid came in carrying a wriggling paper bag. I gave him half a buck and brought the bag into the men's room on the second floor. I gave it a shake and out fell a tiger cat. I had all I could do to keep him from squeezing out the bathroom door. Then in came another kid with a cat in a burlap sack. I took the squirming sack and paid out the fifty cents. Another kid came strolling up, this time with a baby buggy. In it were two more cats in a pillowcase. He got a dollar. I was curious to know how he managed to get two cats. He said he went to a friend's house with the buggy and a pillowcase. He rang the doorbell, knowing his friend wasn't home. The mother answered the door and the boy kept her in conversation until the cat came out in the hallway and onto the porch. When the door closed he snatched the cat and put it into the pillow case and then into the baby buggy. (He was a regular catnapper.) He did the same thing with another friend.

I carried the three cats up to the men's room and tossed them in. By five o'clock, there were sixteen cats—every color, size, and description imaginable—all locked in the second floor men's room.

Publicity for *A Night in Venice* (1929): Larry, Moe, Shemp, Ted Healy.

Now, I must make clear one essential fact. J. J. Shubert was deathly afraid of cats. Monday morning, we all came in for rehearsal, under Shubert's eye. We had just finished with the first sketch when Mr. Shubert started for the men's room. As he opened the door sixteen angry cats jumped him. Shubert fainted. He was taken to the hospital and revived but refused to come back to rehearsal until all the cats were taken away. We called the stage carpenter to build a cage for the cats, and after a struggle, we finally got them into it. We emptied five cans of salmon in with them, just to keep them quiet.

Later, we were transferred to the Century Theater to continue our rehearsals. The cats were carted to the theater and put in the basement. Ted's new idea was to put salmon in our cuffs, so that the cats would follow us on stage during the act. We asked Zwickie, the caretaker for the Stevens Brothers' wrestling bear, to feed the cats for us. We gave him some money, but we didn't know he spent it going to the ball games.

Before long a terrible stench began to permeate the theater. The smell got so bad we had to stop rehearsing. Ted and I went down into the basement and found three of the cats lying dead in the cage. When we opened it, the rest of the cats took off as though they were shot out of a cannon. We gave the dead cats a proper burial and didn't come back to the theater to rehearse until the following Monday. I know for a fact that there were relatives of those cats running around the Century Theater until it closed down many years later.

One of the most unusual stories in show business happened during the run of *A Night in Venice*. The story kept cropping up whenever show folks gathered and was retold for many years thereafter, with some exaggeration along the way.

The show was touring and playing the Grand Theater in Chicago, while on the bill of the Shubert Theater across the street was an Earl Carroll show—I think it was *Sketch Book*. This is how the story was told to me:

It was Thanksgiving eve and a group of showgirls from *Sketch Book* and from *A Night in Venice* were having a high old time at the 606 Club after their performance. In the wee hours the club management raffled off chances on a turkey, and a group of the girls who had pooled their tickets won the twenty-four-pound bird—live, no less! It was packed in a large wooden crate, head protruding and gobbling like mad. The astonished doorman helped the girls put the crate into a cab and off they went to their hotel. With more help, they got the bird into their room and out of the crate. The frightened creature then tore wildly through the suite, under beds, and over tables. The girls were at a loss as to what they should do. One of them had an idea: tie the bird's legs to a chair until morning, at which time they'd cook it. A second girl suggested that they lock it in the closet. A third girl said, "Not with my clothes in there." Finally the girls went into a huddle and came up with a solution. One went to the all-night drugstore on Michigan Avenue where her boyfriend worked, and asked him for some chloroform. She returned to the hotel, chloroformed the bird, gave it a vicious blow over the head, removed the feathers, and put it into the refrigerator.

The next morning, one of the girls went to the refrigerator, opened the door, and that poor featherless gobbler staggered out naked as a newborn bird.

This awesome sight sent the girls screaming down the hall to the apartment of some chorus boys who completed the necessary task of doing away with the bird. A beautiful Thanksgiving dinner was served by the chorus boys in their apartment, but the girls wouldn't eat a thing.

One of our routines in *A Night in Venice* was an act with a wrestling bear. This bear had absolutely no talent other than wrestling any person who held his arms outstretched. It looked quite effective on stage. One of the Stevens Brothers, who owned the bear, would hold it by a halter and strap which was drawn through a ring in its nose, while the other brother and his assistant would each wrestle the animal.

During our act, if either Shemp, Larry, or I came near the bear, it would reach out with its paw, grab us around the ankle and send us sprawling. After flooring Shemp a couple of times and wrestling with the Stevens Brothers, the bear would start to chase us. Larry and I would run across the stage with our pants falling, exposing our brightly colored shorts. The bear, hot on our tail, chased us off stage.

In the wings, hanging on a hook, was a bear hide stuffed with paper, rags, and telephone books. Attached to the bear hide was a long wire which went up into the gridiron through pulleys to the other side of the stage. There was a large ring attached to the wire. Shemp would take the fake bear, enter from the wings and pretend to be struggling with it on stage. Suddenly, he'd throw the bear hide over the heads of the audience, the lights would go out and the bear hide, sailing over the heads of the people in the first few rows, would bring a series of screams. A stagehand would then pull the ring on the wire and bring the hide back on stage.

One time we were doing the show as usual. The Stevens Brothers had finished wrestling, Shemp had taken a few spills, and Larry and I had run on and off the stage a couple of times with our shorts exposed. When we got backstage, Shemp reached for the fake bear hide, took it off the hook and started wrestling. Tripping over his pants, he accidentally let go of the hide which swung loose off stage. Seeing Shemp drop the bear, the stagehand figured the routine was over and walked away from his end of the wire. In the meantime, I saw Shemp fall and drop the hide, so I grabbed it and began struggling with it. I ran with it to the center of the stage and then threw it into the audience. But there was no one on the other end to pull in the slack. There I stood, center stage, and watched this thirty pounds of hide rap itself around three or four heads in the seventh row of the orchestra. I was stunned and so was J. J. Shubert, who had to pay eleven thousand dollars in settlements.

Following our run in *A Night in Venice,* we did our first big-time vaudeville tour on the Loew's circuit. We opened with Ted Healy at Loew's Capitol in Washington, D.C., in late 1929. There were eight acts on the bill with us: a troupe of Arab tumblers and acrobats; the Kennedy Brothers, very accomplished piano players and singers; a comedy act called Willie, West, and McGinty; then Spencer's Dogs. After intermission came a team of adagio dancers, followed by Ted Healy and His Southern Gentlemen: Moe, Shemp and Larry. The Stevens Brothers' wrestling bear appeared with us on stage again, led on by its trainer, followed by Shemp, Larry, and me. The bear started its usual routine by grabbing for my foot and tripping me. Then it proceeded to move its bowels on center stage. The electrician immediately doused the lights, leaving the stage in darkness except for a baby spot on the four of us as we tried to continue our act.

Zwickie, the bearkeeper and cleaner-upper, rushed out with his broom and shovel. Groping in the dark, he began to take care of the bear's mess. The electrician, seeing someone move on stage, hit Zwickie with the second spot. There he stood, open-mouthed, broom and shovel in hand. All he could think of doing was taking a bow. He bent over and the piled up mess slid off the shovel and splattered back on the stage. The audience howled. Healy had his hands full trying to quiet them. Then a fellow in the balcony started to chant, "We want the bear."

Healy stared in the direction of the voice and shouted, "If that's the kind of crap you want, *we'll* give it to you!"

For that line of dialogue, neither Healy nor the three of us could get another Loew's booking for over three years—this after looking forward for so long to working in that gem of circuits. We did get our first booking at the Palace on Broadway, though, in March 1930. *The New York Times* called Healy's Racketeers (Larry, Shemp, and me) "unkempt ruffians and gladiators." The paper's critic said of our act, "It is rough and hardy sport, but unendingly funny."

Getting into Movies and Along Comes Curly

WE MADE OUR FILM DEBUT as a team in 1930. Ted Healy came up with an offer to do a feature film for Fox Studios, the forerunner of Twentieth Century–Fox. The salary was not up to what vaudeville paid at the time, but we were dying to see the palm-lined streets of Hollywood. Healy was to get $1,250 a week and each of us would be paid our now-standard $100. The filming would take five weeks.

I can remember how Ted told us before we started filming, "Boys, one of us or all of us may click in films, so it's the best of luck to anyone who makes it." Our first movie: "Soup to Nuts," an original story and screenplay by Rube Goldberg, the noted cartoonist and inventor. After it was completed, Winnie Sheehan, the head of Fox at the time, came to us with a seven-year contract. Several days later, we were told that Fox had changed its mind and the deal was off. Each of us would be given $500 for expenses and fare back to New York. Not long afterwards, a friend who worked with us during the filming of "Soup to Nuts" told me that he was in Sheehan's office when Ted came in and said, "You know, Mr. Sheehan, you're ruining my act by signing the boys for a contract. I didn't think that one Irishman would do this to another Irishman." Sheehan told him, "Don't be concerned, Ted. I'll take care of this."

When our Fox contract was canceled, we had every intention of rejoining Ted, but when I found out what he'd done, I said to Shemp and Larry, "This is our opportunity to see what we can

MOE HOWARD

Moe as seen by inventor/cartoonist Rube Goldberg, who wrote *Soup to Nuts* (1930).

do as a single act, and I for one am not going back with Ted." We all agreed and the decision was made to go on our own as Howard, Fine, and Howard—Three Lost Souls (I was calling myself Harry Howard at that time). We contacted the William Morris Agency and were immediately booked into the Paramount Theater in Los Angeles for two weeks, followed by one each in Portland and San Francisco.

While rehearsing material for our new act, we took some time to relax by playing a few hands of three-handed bridge. During one hand Larry insisted that he had four honor cards. This was impossible as Shemp and I each had one. Shemp became incensed, and in a fit of anger he stood up, reached over and poked his fingers into Larry's eyes. I started to laugh hysterically and went over backward in my chair. I tried to break my fall by throwing my arm behind me; instead I went crashing through a French door in back of me, smashing the glass and cutting my arm. Larry's eyes were tearing and my arm was bleeding, but I just continued to laugh. The next morning at ten, we opened at the Paramount in Los Angeles. At one point in the act, I said to Larry and Shemp, "Who's the manager of this act?" Walking towards me from my left and right side, they each said, "I am." It was then that I threw my arms out with two fingers on each hand extended and poked both Larry and Shemp in what appeared to be their eyes. The audience erupted and we kept this bit in the act, using it at every performance and in countless films in later years. I never hit them squarely in the eyes, although I did come close a few times.

While we were establishing ourselves as Howard, Fine, and Howard, Ted found himself three other Stooges and got a booking at the Roxy Theater in New York. After his first performance, the manager took him aside: "Ted, you'll ruin yourself working with these three men. They have no sense of timing and don't understand your act. Play sick, and get out of this date." Ted realized he was right and walked out after that first show.

During the next few months, Ted attempted to break up our act. First, he sent Larry an offer to work with him. Larry wired back, "Sorry, Ted, I've signed with Moe and Shemp."

I have recalled and retold this story many times. It happened when we were appearing at an RKO vaudeville house in Kansas City. On the bill with us was Georges Charpentier, the French heavyweight fighter who had made such a good showing against Jack Dempsey for the world championship but, of course, didn't win.

On this particular day, I was in one of my mischievous moods—a hangover from my spitball days—because of the boredom between shows. Since it was terribly hot and humid, I was going to lie down on a cot on the roof of the theater to try to get a tan, while Shemp, Larry, Fred Keating, and Georges Charpentier were sitting on a bench outside the stage door. On my way up to the roof I passed the dressing room door where the girls of the Mangine dance troupe were talking to Fred Keating's young assistant, Anderson. I also noticed a tray of soiled plates and cups on the makeup table and one uneaten piece of blueberry pie. The scene just sort of triggered something. I popped in and asked them if I could have the pie; they told me to take it. I sauntered to the roof and looked over the edge, then back at that wedge of blueberry pie. Below I could see that large, shining bald spot on the top of Larry's head. I leaned over, held the piece of pie in my right hand between my thumb and middle finger, and lined it up with that spot. I just opened my two fingers and let go. It was heavy enough to go straight down without flopping or turning and made a perfect landing smack in the middle of Larry's skull. I ducked back and waited, then slowly started down the stairs.

The Stooges and their wives on the set of *Soup to Nuts*: Shemp and Babe, Moe and Helen, Larry and Mabel.

The team of Howard, Fine and Howard—*Three Lost Souls* (1931).

When Larry got zapped, I later found out, he looked up. The Mangines' dressing room window was open, and Larry, hearing loud laughter coming from the room, rushed in to find the dirty tray with the remaining pieces of blueberry pie. Then he saw Anderson laughing, although Larry didn't realize it had nothing to do with him. Larry simply grabbed a hunk of pie from the top of his head and combed a little out of his hair with his fingers, and jammed part in Anderson's mouth, wiped some on his suit and some on the dressing room walls. The girls screamed at him and Anderson swore. As I reached the landing outside the door, I heard Larry yell, "I wonder where Dead Shot Moe is." When Larry saw me come around the corner, he said, "Okay, Dead Shot, how come the blue on your hand matches the blue on my head?" I told him, "I couldn't help it, Larry. I saw your head shining up at me and since it made such a nice target I just couldn't resist testing my marksmanship."

In spite of the glamour on stage; the beauty of the chandeliers hanging over the audience, the heavily upholstered seats, the plush carpeting throughout the theater, the elaborate gold-leaf encrustations decorating the walls, elaborate box offices, and smart display cases for posters and photographs of the performers, the backstage area in the majority of the theaters, we found, was most unappealing.

The dressing rooms were unclean, unheated, unventilated, and rat-infested. In some of the theaters, the manager used the dressing room as a storeroom, often filled with bags of unpopped corn, sometimes up to the ceiling. The bottom bags usually had holes where the rats were nibbling. In other dressing rooms, they'd store the machines used to pop the corn. The few dressing rooms available to the performers were generally inadequate for the number of those appearing on the bill. The average room had a metal shelf for makeup, a sink with cold water (some performers would use it as a urinal rather than walk the vast distances to the toilets), a large mirror usually

The Racketeers—and Ted Healy (1932).

Curly Howard in a rare film apart from the Stooges, with George Givot and Joe Callahan in MGM's Technicolor musical revue, *Roast Beef and Movies* (1933).

Ted Healy, Fred Sanborn, Larry, Moe and Shemp in *Soup to Nuts*.

Howard, Fine and Howard in lights for the first time—at the RKO Orpheum in Seattle (1931).

hung over the makeup shelf, if you were lucky, a few chairs and a cot, and a bare white bulb on the ceiling to add to the dismal atmosphere.

One day our wives decided to surprise us and dress up our dressing room, so they bought some brightly colored flowered chintz and made covers for the chairs, a scarf for the makeup shelf, and a curtain to place in front of the bare rod that held our clothes. When we came off stage, we thought we were in the wrong room. Then we saw our wives giggling among themselves and knew we'd been redecorated. Unfortunately, the joy didn't last long, for we had to gather up our decorations when we moved to the next theater, and somehow we never took the trouble to put them up again.

There were always exceptions to the rule, and the Cleveland Palace in the RKO circuit was one of them. This theatre was built without missing a thought for the actors' comfort. The Palace was beautiful not only outside and in the auditorium, but also backstage. Most impressive was the second floor of the theater, which sported a regulation-size pool table, chess tables, comfortable chairs, an ice machine and soft drinks, playing cards, cigars—it had all the facilities of a private club. In the basement was a laundry room complete with washing machines—no dryers in those days—while on the third floor were lines to spread and dry clothes, and warm air was piped in. There was even a nursery for youngsters. Best of all were the dressing rooms, heavily carpeted with mirrored walls and makeup tables. They had everything in them, right down to padded coat hangers.

It was during 1931 that we hired as our straight man Jack Walsh, a handsome Irishman with black hair, baby blue eyes, and thick, sensuous lips. Jack had a fair singing voice as well as a more fantastic technique as a liar than Baron Munchausen.

Once, while sitting with Shemp in a coffee shop near the Oriental Theater in Chicago, I overheard Jack talking to a young lady in the booth behind us. He was trying to entice her up to his room with an extraordinary line: about how his family had cornered the market on Coca-Cola bottle caps and had machinery that could make old caps as good as new. Jack got her up to his room to talk over some secretarial work that he had for her—with Coca-Cola, of course. She stayed in his room with him for a week, and when we left town, he gave her a gift and told her that when he returned to Chicago he wanted to talk marriage with her—that is, if his parents would let him. Right now, he explained, they needed him at work—at the company they owned that made the straps that people hold onto in the subway cars; they rented these straps out to the subway company for six dollars a month. They had fifteen thousand of them in all, and his parents wanted him to take over the company.

The boys back with Ted Healy in 1932.

The boys off-guard, with Larry's wife, Mabel (left), and Moe's wife, Helen.

Larry, Ted, Moe and Curly push the specialty of the house in *Beer and Pretzels* (1933).

On another occasion, we were invited to the home of a very prominent theater executive. At coffee time, Jack started talking about his "college days," though I don't believe he graduated from grade school. He explained that he was studying animal husbandry and told how his mother had urged him to rush home recently. There was something terribly wrong with their Poodle, Hercules. Jack told how he took the next train home and arrived early in the morning to find Hercules turning in circles and grabbing frantically at his tail. After a thorough examination, Jack decided that it was imperative to operate immediately. He slit Hercules's tail open and found the trouble. It seemed that Hercules had eaten some grass on which there were snake eggs, which then hatched and grew full size. Snakes were eating their way through the dog's tail! At this point, Jack opened his jacket and displayed his snakeskin belt from "that" snake, and told how there was enough left for suspenders and a purse for his mother.

These stories flowed out endlessly, but one in particular I shall never forget. We were playing Chicago, and after one show Shemp, Jack, and I went to dinner. At the restaurant, Jack ordered fried chicken. When they served it, he picked up a wing, spread it out, and sniffed. He pushed his plate away from him and said to the waiter, "You know, I remember the time I was helping my grandmother on the streetcar. I was on the step just below her when that car started with a jerk and my grandmother lurched backward. Her behind landed on my face, and you know I never smelled anything like that until I smelled this chicken."

MGM's two-reel Technicolor musical revue, *Hello Pop* (1933), which starred
Ted Healy and his Stooges, Howard, Fine and Howard — as the credits read.

Embarrassed, Shemp and I quickly paid our check and left the restaurant without eating. So
much for Jack Walsh. He was quite a straight man and the whole world was his Stooge.

I experienced my first involvement with racism in the business when we played Jacksonville,
Florida, in 1931. I knew there was segregation in the southern theaters, but was not fully aware of
the pain that it caused until then. After moving our trunks, scenery, and baggage into the vaudeville house in Jacksonville, I went backstage and looked the theater over. I asked the doorman to
show me to my dressing room and I put my attaché case containing our music on a chair in the
room, closed the door, and went to find out the rehearsal schedule and when our scenery would be
hung. I was told that we had plenty of time, so I decided to take a walk. Outside the stage door, four
stagehands and the music conductor smiled at me as I passed. As I came to the corner, I saw a
black man of about eighty coming toward me. When he reached me, he jumped out into the gutter. Thinking he'd seen a snake or something frightening, I jumped into the road with him, whereupon he jumped back onto the sidewalk, and so did I. We did this dance routine about three times
before I finally grabbed his arm and said, "What the hell is going on, pop? Why are you leaping up
and back like a jumping jack?" Frightened, he answered, "Sir, in this city a black man musn't walk
on the same side of the street with a white man." "Mister," I told him, "this is not my city, but it's
my country and I can walk with any man I choose to." I put my arm about his shoulder and forced

him to walk with me around the corner. He said, "Man, you seem nice, but you're liable to get us killed." I tried to calm him, and then let him go his way while I continued my walk.

When I went back to the theater, I found the stagehands and music conductor still sitting by the stage door. When I spoke to them about getting our scenery up, they not only wouldn't talk to me but wouldn't even look at me. Shemp and Larry came over from the hotel and I told them that it looked like trouble with the stagehands. By this time, the curtain was down and people were coming into the theater.

We went around to the front of the theater and found that our pictures were taken out of the frames and our names were painted out. Puzzled, we asked the manager what the hell was wrong, why the stage hands wouldn't move our scenery, why the conductor wouldn't talk to us. He explained that the stagehands had seen me walking down the street with my arms around "a nigger," and then informed us, "Your baggage and trunks have gone back to the station; here is your music, and salary check. We don't want any nigger lovers in our theater or in our city, so get movin' before you get in *big* trouble."

We left Jacksonville in disbelief. When we arrived back in New York, we told the story to our agent and to the newspapers and that was that—until forty years later.

I was coming out of the Safeway market in West Hollywood when a tall, heavy-set man came up to me and said that the manager of the market told him that I was Moe Howard of the Three Stooges. He wanted to know if I was one of the three fellows who had played Jacksonville many years ago. When I told him I was, he said, "I'm so glad I ran into you, I've always wanted to apologize for playing you dirty in Jacksonville. I was one of the stagehands who wouldn't hang your scenery for walking with the black man. I had to go along with them or lose my job. Please forgive me." He walked away smiling after I gave him an autographed photo of The Three Stooges.

Moe and Curly welcome their parents to sunny California in 1933.

The Stooges and Ted clown with Clark Gable on the set of *Dancing Lady* (1933).

In *Meet the Baron* (1933), the boys and Ted threaten the dignity of Edna May Oliver.

We completed several weeks on the Coast and were booked into the Hippodrome in New York. At this point, I finally recognized Ted's Jekyll and Hyde personality—his deceitful ways, the way he had subjugated us, the pittance he'd paid us. I had been his closest friend for years as well as his advisor and constant shadow. I'd tried to protect him while he was drinking heavily. In return, he threatened the Hippodrome Theater with a lawsuit if they let us appear on stage using "his" material—which, if it belonged to anyone, was the property of J. J. Shubert. After Ted's threats, the management asked us if we had any other material we could use—we did—but I finally went to J. J. Shubert for help. I knew he was on our side, as Ted recently had tried to sue him.

Mr. Shubert was a gentleman. He told me, "Moe, I'm drawing up a paper allowing you and the boys to use any jokes, scenes, or material that you wish to from the plays *A Night in Venice* and *A Night in Spain*." Armed with that paper, I went to the manager of the Hippodrome, who made a photocopy of it. He also had me seat a stenographer in the audience and have her copy our dialogue word for word and describe the action in our routine. Then he had the papers notarized.

The act had been put together hastily and didn't go over too well in the early days of our engagement, but by the end of the week, after three shows a day, there was a vast improvement, and the continuation of our booking as Howard, Fine, and Howard told us we were being received quite well. Healy's underhanded tricks to break us up continued. He hired some toughs from Chicago who threatened us with bodily injury and assorted broken limbs if we went on working. We ignored the threats, and luckily nothing happened. Maybe they liked our act.

An annoyed Ted allows the boys to make their point in *Meet the Baron*.

The Stooges give the old raspberry to Jimmy Durante, Jack Pearl and Ted Healy in *Meet the Baron*.

Ted and the Stooges address the crowd before taking off in *Plane Nuts* (1933).

Then came a hiatus in Ted's war against us. He was floundering with his three new men in Billy Rose's new musical *Crazy Quilt*, and was drinking more than he could handle—not showing up regularly for all his performances. He was suffering from a bad case of the DT's. When I heard of his troubles, I asked Larry to come with me to Ted's hotel; Shemp couldn't bring himself to go. We found Ted in his room, screaming. He insisted there were firemen coming through the walls of his room. It took us hours to straighten Ted out so he could do the evening performance, and after the show, we spent half the night in his room with him.

We were appearing at the Oriental Theater in Chicago that month, and Healy begged us to go back with him, complaining that he had no act without us.

"Ted," I told him, "finish the run of your show for Billy Rose and then we'll talk about rejoining you."

He replied, "But the show doesn't close for another four months."

I said, "That's the way it'll have to be. Cut out the booze and we'll get together in early January. *Our* contracts have about twelve weeks to run, and we'll wait for you to finish the Rose show—if you're still on the wagon."

Healy promised us he'd stay off the booze; it was one of the few promises he kept—for a while. But when we were to rejoin him, Shemp just wouldn't go along.

"Moe," he said to me, "Ted is not the wonderful guy you think he is; he's basically an alcoholic. He's only one drink from going back to his terrifying benders. Besides, I have a chance to play the part of Knobby Walsh in a Joe Palooka film for Vitaphone on the Coast."

Matthew Betz appears to be intimidated by Ted, Bonnie Bonnell and the boys in *Plane Nuts*.

Curly, Ted, Bonnie, Larry and Moe get one of the props ready in *Dancing Lady,* one of the MGM features they made in 1933.

Curly, Moe and Larry with Robert Montgomery during a break in *Fugitive Lovers* (1934).

The next day when I told Ted about Shemp's opportunity to do a film, Healy blew his top, shouting, "What the hell does Shemp mean by that! Is he trying to ruin my act? I need a drink!"

Losing my patience, I said, "Ted, if you take a drink, it'll be the last time you'll ever see me again."

He calmed down, and then wanted to know what we were going to do about replacing Shemp. I explained that we'd send for my kid brother, Jerome.

As a young man, Jerome (later Curly) was an accomplished ballroom dancer, spending much of his time at the Triangle Ballroom in Brooklyn breezing gracefully over the dance floor, sometimes rubbing shoulders with the future greats like George Raft. During his teens, Curly usually was the life of any party. He had a beautiful singing voice and was a very nice-looking young man with his wavy chestnut-brown hair. Being ten years younger than me, he was really considered the baby of the family, and we had gone our separate ways.

In 1928, he joined Orville Knapp's band as a comedy conductor. He had a full head of wavy hair and a wax-tipped mustache and wore tails which were made to break away piece by piece as he conducted the band. As he moved his arms, waving the baton gracefully, one sleeve and then the other would fall from his coat. After a few more motions of his baton, the coat would split in half down the back. Finally the pants would break away, and he would be left conducting in long underwear with a drop seat that was held up with a horse blanket pin. At that moment the band would close with a roll of drums and a crash of symbols, and he'd bow and leave the stage, always to a roar of laughter.

He left Orville Knapp in 1932 to join Ted Healy, Larry, and me. In vaudeville days, after he finished the act for the evening, the night clubs were his home. Curly always loved music, and a drum beat or an old song would start his foot tapping. Many times at his favorite night spot, when he was feeling no pain, he would take the tablecloth between his fingers and just tear it in two to the tempo of the music or take two spoons and click them together with an unbelievable beat. Sometimes he would jump up on the bandstand, grab the bass fiddle, and join the band—and do it well. I remember going around to the various clubs the day after paying for the damage he'd done. I would worry whenever he was late coming home, staying awake in my room half the night waiting for him. When I heard his voice yelling, "Swing it," I knew he was back in the hotel and I could go to sleep.

Curly had four unsuccessful marriages and two children, at least a dozen homes, and a new car every year, but his obsession was his love for dogs. In nearly every city we played, he would buy another one. An Irish setter, a boxer, a kerry blue, a collie—you name it and Curly would buy it. He would keep the dog with him for a week or two, then ship it home to Los Angeles from wherever we were playing.

Shortly after my brother joined our act, Ted called us together and said, "Larry, you have a head like a wild porcupine. You, Moe, have a spittoon haircut. But Jerome, with your wavy hair

The boys relax with Bonnie and Ted between films at MGM.

and wax-tipped mustache, you just don't fit in." He asked Ted to adjourn our meeting for twenty minutes. Exactly twenty minutes later, he was back—without his mustache and wearing a cap pulled down tightly over his ears. He looked and walked like a fat fairy. Then he whipped off the cap. I stared, astounded: he had shaved his head to look like a dirty tennis ball.

"You're in," Healy laughed.

With tears rolling down his cheeks, my brother said, "If you want me, call me Curly." He said this while rubbing his hand over his smooth dome. And Curly he was from that time on.

In 1932, we were in New York to start another vaudeville tour. Ted was staying at the Park Crescent, a very posh hotel. He had booked us into the New Yorker Café in the basement of the old Christie Hotel in Hollywood. It was a new low for Ted. He had just been divorced and had no money to pay his hotel bill, let alone fare to Hollywood for six people. Our booking agency agreed to advance Ted for our fares, and he was to leave for the Coast in three days—a sixty-hour trip by train. The problem now was how to get his clothes and those of his girlfriend out of the hotel. And his tails and evening clothes were in a trunk in the hotel's basement.

Ted already owed the hotel twelve hundred dollars' rent, and he knew that the management would never let him take his clothes out of the hotel. So I devised a scheme. Ted's apartment was on the twenty-eighth floor, one floor below the roof. I got three of my friends to help us, and had three cabs wait for us outside of the apartment. I went up to Ted's place with a friend and stuffed all of Ted's girlfriend's lingerie under my belt and the waistband of my pants and put on two of Ted's jackets. My friend did the same thing. We came out of the elevator and did an off-to-Buffalo shuffle through the lobby and into one of the cabs. We were followed by Larry and another friend repeating our act and depositing their things into a second cab. Next came Curly and one of his friends, loaded with more of Ted's clothes. They did a cute dance out the door as the clerk waved to them. Several trips later, I was wearing Ted's camel's-hair coat. He was six foot two and I was five foot four. As I passed the clerk with Ted's coat wrapped under my chin, I made a pretty weird picture.

Next was the problem of Ted's evening wear that was in the trunk in the basement. He went to the manager and told him he'd like to get his trunk from the basement. Of course he refused. Ted then offered a deal: "Look, here's my contract for two-thousand seven-hundred and fifty dollars a week. I can't go to work without my tails and evening clothes. How can you expect me to pay back rent if I can't go to work?" The manager thought better of it and told Ted that he could take the evening clothes out of the trunk but nothing else. That was fine since there was nothing else in it. Ted returned to his apartment, put his evening clothes in a bag together with his comb and toothbrush, and then went up to the roof with a tremendously heavy beaver lap robe. I was standing in the street twenty-eight stories below and finally spotted Ted's bald head peeking over the rooftop. He raised the robe high over his head and tossed it. The robe weaved from side to side clumsily as the wind caught it, wrapping around a flagpole outside of the fifth floor. It made a very impressive and expensive flag blowing in the wind. Ted naturally was very upset that he had lost his lap robe, but I reminded him that at least we had his stage clothes. I remember thinking, "The show must go on," and I started to hum, "California here I come."

A few days after our opening at the New Yorker Café in Hollywood, Larry and I were playing cards in our apartment at the Lido Hotel when all hell broke loose. The building started to shake like a house of cards.

Larry's eyes bugged. "What the devil is that?"

I said, "That's got to be an earthquake."

Larry replied, "What the hell are we doing sitting here?" and bounded out of the apartment, running smack into Curly who was pounding on Ted's door, yelling, "Come on now, Ted, cut that out!"

Curly was certain that Ted, whose apartment was right above his own, was up to one of his old tricks. I screamed to Curly to get out of the building fast, as we were in the middle of an earthquake. The three of us pushed Ted's door open, and there he was—arms spread apart under a doorway, poised like Atlas trying to hold up the world. Unable to get Ted to move from his spot, we three decided to try for the basement. Rushing through the lobby, we saw an enormous crystal chandelier—more than three hundred pounds of tinkling, flashing prisms—swaying on its chains from one side of the lobby to the other. This was certainly a frightening sight. The main shocks and aftershocks lasted about an hour with milder shocks continuing for days.

That night at the club, we had two shows to do. Everything went along smoothly for about fifteen minutes at the early show; then came a rather sharp aftershock. We quit in midjoke and raced from the club, along with most of the customers. I found myself standing in the middle of Hollywood Boulevard, afraid to stand too close to the buildings, pieces of which were falling to the sidewalk. High atop one of the buildings nearby was a round cupola with about six oval niches, each containing a statue. As each shock wave rolled beneath me, the statues would lean out of their niches and then sway back. I was still in the middle of the street when a large convertible came straight for me. I jumped aside. The driver shouted at me to get out of the street, and I yelled back, "It's an earthquake, you idiot!"

I heard him shout, "Sorry!" as he took off as though shot out of a cannon.

After about ten minutes, the commotion subsided, and some of us went back into the club. Many never did return, though. Others came back and paid their bills. Some paid by check, which we found impossible to cash—the banks were closed. Anyway, we finished the act, but this wasn't time for laughter. The audience had dwindled to about twenty from the original two hundred. We hung around the club until the scheduled late show; finally the manager said, "It's no use!" We accepted half salary and went home.

My wife Helen was back in New York at the time with our daughter Joan, and I tried to explain to her about the near-catastrophe. That was a mistake, as I had a difficult time later trying to get her to return to California.

In MGM's *Hollywood Party* (1934), Larry, Moe, Ted and Curly threaten champion Max Baer and his date, Mary Carlisle.

Wallace Beery drops by the set, where the boys are starting to create havoc.

A short time after the New Yorker Café date, Harry Rapf of MGM asked us to do a charity benefit at the Uplifters' Ranch and signed us—and Ted—to a one-year contract at the studio.

During 1933, we made five two-reel comedies with Ted at MGM, two in color. *Hello Pop* was one. We also did *Plane Nuts*, an airplane story in which we flew around the world upside down and backwards; *Beer and Pretzels*, a musical short by Gus Kahn; and *The Big Idea*, a musical revue. Later Larry, Curly, Ted, and I made four or five features for the studio, including *Meet The Baron*, starring Jack Pearl as the Baron Munchausen. Jimmy Durante and ZaSu Pitts were also in this one. We also made *Turn Back the Clock* with Lee Tracy and Mae Clarke; *Fugitive Lovers*, with Madge Evans and Robert Montgomery; *Dancing Lady* with Joan Crawford, Clark Gable, and Franchot Tone; and *Hollywood Party* with Lupe Velez, Jimmy Durante, Laurel and Hardy, Jack Pearl, and others.

In early May 1934, after *Hollywood Party*, we came to a final parting of the ways with Ted. We were walking through the vast MGM complex when we came face to face with him and his agent, Paul Dempsey.

I said, "Ted, I saw your latest film, 'Death on the Diamond' (he had made a half dozen without us Stooges) and at least four times during the picture you extended your arms as if you were pushing us back. You always did that when we worked with you as Stooges. Only this time we weren't there and it made you look very awkward."

Dempsey nodded. "You know, Ted, Moe is right, I noticed that, too." Then I continued, "In all honesty, Ted, you really don't need us any longer. You're doing great on your own. Let's sign a paper right here stating that, as of this date, we will go our separate ways."

Ted looked at Dempsey, who agreed: "Moe knows what he's talking about. I'll draw up the paper and you'll each sign a copy." In no time, he was back with the releases, and it took us less time to sign them. Larry, Curly, and I wished Ted every success and the three of us walked away.

Finally, alone, both Larry and Curly jumped on me: "Gosh, Moe, why did you do that? What are we going to do now?"

I said, "Listen, boys, if we stick with Ted we'll be getting our measly one hundred dollars a week. Let's see what we can do on our own. No more of that Howard, Fine, and Howard. Right now we are *three* fairly good comics, and we were Healy's *Stooges*, so let's call ourselves—THE THREE STOOGES!"

The Final Break with Ted Healy

ON THE DAY WE LEFT MGM after breaking with Ted Healy, I tried to convince Larry and Curly that there had to be a place for us in the movie industry. We found our place, but through a veritable comedy of errors.

We each had come to MGM that day in our own cars. As we were ready to go our separate ways, Larry reminded me, "Don't forget, Moe, we'll meet later this afternoon at your apartment."

While walking toward my car, I was stopped by a young man, Walter Kane, an agent. He told me that he had seen the three of us with Ted Healy, and that if I would accompany him to Columbia Studios, he felt he could get the Stooges a contract. Mr. Kane and I went directly to Columbia and, without an appointment, he brought me in to meet studio head Harry Cohn and production chief Sam Briskin, who told me that they had seen the Stooges work with Ted at the New Yorker Café and that Columbia would like to sign us to a one-picture deal. After sixty days, if they liked what they saw they would give us a long-term contract.

Cohn said, "Of course, you must understand the film will be a two-reel comedy, not a feature. We're willing to pay you fifteen hundred dollars for the first short."

Woman Haters (1934), the Stooges' first Columbia two-reeler, finds the boys thinking they are taking advantage of Marjorie White.

Dorothy Grainger leads on both Moe and Curly in *Punch Drunks* (1934).

In *Punch Drunks*, Al Hill prepares to finish off Curly, braced by Moe.

All this sounded fair to me, and I agreed to the figures while they sent for someone from the legal department to draw up a temporary paper stating the salary, the starting date, and the sixty-day-approval clause.

Meanwhile, Larry left MGM about the same time as I had, only a different young man—an agent named Joe Rivkin—approached him.

"Larry, I've been watching you boys work with Ted Healy for some time. I heard that you've left Ted."

Larry said, "Boy, the news sure travels fast!"

Rivkin talked Larry into going with him to Universal Studios, in the valley, where Rivkin told him, he could get the Stooges a film contract—provided Larry had the right to sign for the group. Larry assured Rivkin he had the authority, so off they went to the office of Carl Laemmle, Jr., head man at Universal.

After introductions and a short discussion of terms, Laemmle sent for a studio lawyer and a form contract was drawn up for the Three Stooges. The legal department stamped it with the date and hour, and Larry signed it.

The boys try to intercept a broken-field runner in *Three Little Pigskins* (1934).

The Stooges' Oscar-nominated short, *Men in Black* (1934), with Ruth Hiatt as the nurse and Charles King as the anesthesiologist.

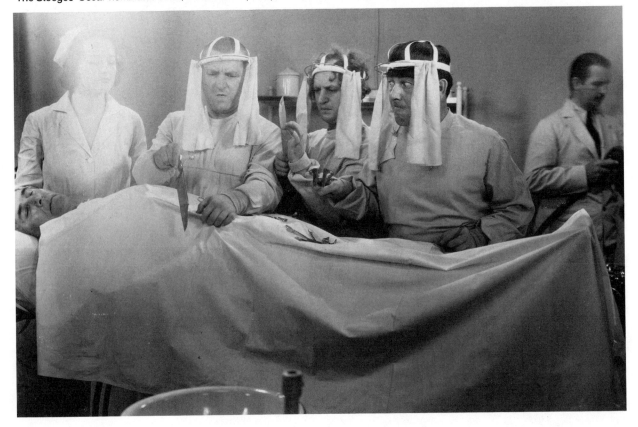

The cast of *The Captain Hates the Sea* (1934). The Stooges are at the captain's table with Alison Skipworth, "Captain" Walter Connelly, Wynne Gibson, Emily Fitzroy and Donald Meek. Standing: John Wray, G. Pat Collins, Arthur Treacher, Leon Errol, John Gilbert, director Lewis Milestone, author Wallace Smith, Victor McLaglen, Akim Tamiroff, Walter Catlett and Claude Gillingwater.

Later, when I met with Larry and Curly in my apartment I said, "Boys, we've accomplished what I was hoping for, a contract at Columbia Pictures."

Then Larry piped up, "A contract with Columbia? I've just signed one at Universal!"

The next morning, I went back to Columbia, asked to see Mr. Cohn, and explained to him what had happened with Larry. "You know, Moe,"—he laughed—"this story would make a helluva movie." Then he called in the head of the legal department. We looked at the agreement and checked the time stamped on it. He then phoned Universal and asked their legal department what time Larry signed his agreement. I couldn't hear what they answered, but Mr. Cohn hung up, turned to me, and said, "You boys belong to Columbia!"

Several years later, Universal signed Abbott and Costello. I doubt very much if they would have joined Universal if fate had us sign there first. Years before, when we were starring at the Steel Pier in Atlantic City, Abbott and Costello were appearing there in a minstrel show, and at every opportunity, they would come backstage and watch us perform from the wings. I always felt there was much of Curly—his mannerisms and high-pitched voice—in Costello's act in feature films.

We made our first two-reel comedy for Columbia, *Woman Haters*, in late June 1934. It was a musical, all in rhyme, written and directed by the songwriter, Archie Gottler. Actually the three of us appeared in the film separately, not as a team.

Moe in a heart-to-heart talk with his "son" in *Three Little Pigskins*.

The finish of a barroom brawl, Three Stooges style, in *Horse Collars* (1935).

The boys — and friend — in a familiar Three Stooges pose.

Our contract stated that the studio had the right to wait sixty days after the film was completed before they exercised their option to sign us to a long-term deal. Larry and Curly were pleased, but after going over the deal at my leisure, I was bothered. I just didn't like the idea of having to wait a month before starting a second comedy, and I put down on paper an idea I had in mind for a long time: a story called *Punch Drunks.* It took me two nights and a day to complete the nine-page treatment; then I had a stenographer type it for me. I showed it to the boys and they agreed it was good. I made an appointment with Ben Kahane, a Columbia executive, for the following morning. Our agent at the time was Leo Morrison, but I felt that I had to take care of this appointment myself. The next morning I acted out the entire story for Kahane while he watched— all smiles.

When I finished, he said, "It's great. You've really sold me. I'll take this up with Mr. Cohn and Mr. Briskin at our meeting today." I thanked him and left.

Two days later, Kahane called. "Moe," he said, "I have some good news for you. Bring the boys with you and come to my office at two-thirty this afternoon." Curly and Larry met me in front of the studio. I couldn't wait to get into Kahane's office to hear the news but I decided that we should be a little late so we wouldn't seem too anxious.

At exactly 2:32 we entered. Mr. K. was smiling, so all I could do was smile in return, although my heart was thumping like mad. "Moe," he said, "the studio is not going to wait the sixty days after *Woman Haters* to make a decision on your contract. I'm having my secretary type up another agreement. We're going to shoot *Punch Drunks* right away, and we're giving you a seven-

The Stooges demonstrate their gunslinging techniques to Old West saloon gals in *Horse Collars*.

Curly, Larry and Moe try on their sleuthing outfits in *Horse Collars*.

Curly gets up out of turn and is bopped on the head by Moe and Larry in *Restless Knights* (1935).

year contract with yearly options. You will be required to make eight two-reel comedies in a forty-week period with a twelve-week layoff to do what you wish—except make films elsewhere. Your salary will be seventy-five hundred per film, making a yearly total of sixty thousand dollars."

We were thrilled at the time with this fantastic offer but didn't realize the ramifications of this contract.

Although television was far in the distance, our contract contained a clause that stipulated that Columbia Pictures Corporation shall have the rights to use our voices and our likenesses as well as our film product in perpetuity in mediums existing now or to be invented. This clause shut the door to any royalty payments when the 194 Columbia shorts we were to make were later released to television. A few years after the TV release of our shorts, Ronald Reagan, then president of the Screen Actors Guild, was instrumental in passing an SAG ruling that there would be no residuals for pictures made prior to 1960. This shut us out again.

We had a worthwhile clause in the contract, which gave us twelve weeks off each year to work where and at whatever we wished. And we could keep all we earned on our personal appearance tours—and on many occasions we worked as much as twenty weeks.

At least one of the boys seems to be out of uniform in *Restless Knights*.

The boys run amok in an artists' studio in *Pop Goes the Easel* (1935).

The clay-slinging climax begins in *Pop Goes the Easel.*

Although we were with Columbia for over twenty-four years, our contract was lucrative—for them and us. Columbia made millions from the Stooges, although they put us through the wringer each time our option came up.

I believe it was the waiting each year, sometimes until the last moment, for Columbia to pick up our option for an additional year that was so upsetting to me and my family. And I found it had a great deal to do with breaking down my self-confidence. After the second option was picked up, Mr. Kahane told us, "Boys, it's really getting tough to sell two-reel comedies. Movie houses in the South are going into double features and they only have room for two features, a one-reel cartoon, and a newsreel. There's no place for two-reelers."

The studio painted a dire picture for the future of Stooges comedies. Then came that heart-breaking wait on the third option, which was finally picked up. The next year brought more frustrating dialogue about two-reel comedies not being too acceptable, then more waiting. I finally began to understand the studio's psychology—to keep us off-balance, to keep us from asking for an increase in salary. And it worked.

Years later, I found out that the Stooges' films were always in tremendous demand all over the country. In visiting several of the Columbia film exchanges, I was told by the bookers that when a theater manager came in for a Stooges comedy he was forced to take one of Columbia's "B" pictures. After that I realized how the studio had deceived us.

We suffered through the first seven years and then learned that the studio had another clause to continue the contract for an additional fourteen years with yearly options.

Our contract with Columbia ended, finally, in 1958. We were there for twenty-four years,

In *Uncivil Warriors* (1935), Curly, Moe and Larry confound officer James C. Morton.

the longest for any team in Hollywood. We walked out without fanfare, knowing it was a job well done. And that we had a following of millions of wonderful and loyal fans.

During our association with Columbia we starred in 194 shorts and 5 feature-length films. For our work in shorts we were nominated once for an Academy Award (for *Men In Black*) and received the Exhibitor's Laurel Awards for being top two-reel moneymakers for the years 1950, 1951, 1952, 1953 and 1954.

After four decades these films are still being shown in every part of the world.

Our first comedy at Columbia, *Woman Haters,* had a scene in a Pullman car in which Walter Brennan had a bit as a train conductor. This was one of his earliest films, and he had a difficult time learning his lines. The picture was a musical and the song he had to do was spoken rather than sung. In this comedy Larry broke his finger tumbling out of the upper berth.

In our second film, *Punch Drunks,* Curly had to appear in the ring with a professional fighter, and he came away with a bloody nose and a cut lip. And Larry, too, had his troubles. In one scene, he is running through the streets looking for someone who was playing the tune *Pop Goes the Weasel.* He comes to a truck with a man on the back waiting to make a speech. Larry hops into the truck, drives off. The man on the back somersaulted off and broke his arm.

In the film *Men in Black,* a take-off on Clark Gable's hit *Men in White,* we were cut by flying glass when we slammed a glass door in one of the hospital scenes.

Three Little Pigskins, our first football film, was a humdinger of bangs and bruises. The young Lucille Ball was excellent in this one in the role of a gun moll. In one scene Curly is running along the sideline for a touchdown, while Larry and I are blocking for him. (I must mention that all the football players, except us, were from Loyola University. They knew how to tackle and they tackled hard.) During the touchdown run, the four (actor) news photographers on the sidelines try to get us to stop for a picture, whereupon Curly, Larry, and I are pounced on by the entire Loyola team. The boys and I reviewed this scene and we could see nothing but trouble with these two-hundred-pounders landing on top of us. Larry called over director Raymond McCarey and said, "Look, we can't do this scene. We're not stuntmen and if one of these gorillas falls on us, we'll never be able to finish the picture. We've never used doubles before but we certainly need them now."

McCarey told us, "Listen, fellows, you know how to take falls. You've done enough of them. It'll take hours to find doubles for you. Besides, we can't afford them. Don't worry, you won't get hurt." I agreed, "You're darn right we won't get hurt. We're not doing the scene."

Forty-five minutes later McCarey had the three doubles on the field and ten minutes after that they were in uniform, wearing wigs which the prop man located. With cameras rolling, Curly ran along the sidelines, and Larry and I were blocking. Then the football players charged toward us, the four news cameramen yelled, "Hold it for a picture," and we stopped to pose. The camera cut and moved into a long shot as our doubles came in. All of the players, including the doubles, landed in a heap on top of the newsmen. When they came up for air, two of the doubles had bro-

Larry, Moe and Curly are the McSnort Brothers in *Pardon My Scotch* (1935), but Pauline High tries to ignore the proceedings.

The boys try a new tactic: to scare a salary increase from boss Harry Cohn at Columbia.

Kitty McHugh appears strangely at ease among the Stooges in *Hoi Polloi* (1935).

80

The boys mix rubbish with high society in *Hoi Polloi*.

ken legs, all four newsmen had broken arms or legs, and all wound up in the hospital—except for the double who stood for Curly. He was padded all over to resemble Curly and the padding broke the blows.

McCarey was speechless and sat in his director's chair with his head in his hands.

In *Ants in the Pantry* in 1936, we played exterminators who turn up at a swanky party. There was a scene where we were having trouble selling our services, so we complain to our boss, who tells us, "If they don't have any bugs, *give* them some!" We got the idea and went from house to house throwing moths in with minks, mice on the floor, and ants in the pantry. During the shooting, I hadn't noticed that a small container of red ants had broken apart in my pocket and the little devils were crawling down my back, in my hair, and into my pants. It was insane. All through the scene I was scratching and squirming and slapping myself on my neck and face and on the seat of my pants. Elated, director Preston Black shouted, "Great Moe. Keep up that squirming!" It was very funny—to everyone but me.

In one of my favorite comedies, *A Pain in the Pullman*, also made in 1936, we played the parts of actors working as vaudevillians. The film took place aboard a train, and in one sequence, all three of us wound up in the same upper berth. Later, we found ourselves a drawing room, not knowing it was assigned to the star of the show. There was a lovely table set in the room with all kinds of delicacies.

A society party in *Hoi Polloi* ends in true Three Stooges fashion.

At one point Curly picked up a hard-shell Dungeness crab. We, of course, were not supposed to know what it was. Curly thought it was a tarantula, Larry figured it to be an octopus, and I concluded that it must be something to eat or it wouldn't be on the table with crackers and sauce.

As the scene progressed, Curly tried to open the crab shell and bent the tines of his fork. I took the fork from Curly, tossed a napkin on the floor, and asked him to pick it up. When Curly bent over, I hit him on the head with the crab, breaking the shell into a million pieces. Then Curly scooped out some of the meat, tasted it, and made a face. He threw the meat away and proceeded to eat the shell.

I have to tell you, if there's one thing to which I have an aversion, it's shellfish, and I couldn't bring myself—even for a film—to put that claw in my mouth. Preston Black, the director, asked me to just lick the claw but I couldn't. He finally had the prop man duplicate the claw out of sugar and food coloring and had me nibble on it as though I was enjoying it. I was still very wary during the scene. I was afraid they had coated the real shell with sugar and that that awful claw was underneath. I chewed that claw during the scene, but if you'll notice, I did it very gingerly.

In the meantime Curly was still chewing on the shell, which was cutting the inside of his mouth. Finally our star comes back to his room and kicks us out, and we three climb into our upper berth to go to sleep. During the scene Larry started snoring loud enough to be heard through the train. I yelled, "Hey, Larry, wake up and go to sleep."

My childhood accuracy with pea-shooters, spitballs, and penny-pitching became helpful in the years when we were making two-reel comedies at Columbia Pictures. I was called on countless times by the producer or director whenever there was an object to be thrown either on screen or from off camera. Our producer one day figured that I had saved the studio thousands of dollars in time and film by my accurate aim with pies, cakes, cream puffs, and assorted gunk that bombarded my fellow actors.

Their popularity commands special marquee billing for The Three Stooges in their theater appearances. Here, they play the RKO Palace in Seattle in 1936.

Movie-making a la the Stooges in *Movie Maniacs* (1936). ▶

An annoyed Moe sets up Larry and Curly for a little head-bopping in *Ants in the Pantry* (1936).

The boys — out of costume and makeup, circa 1936.

Shemp as Knobby Walsh in one of his Joe Palooka shorts for Vitaphone, *Here's Howe* (1936). Blond Robert Norton is Palooka and Beverly Phalen his girl.

Several starlets charm Moe into giving them screen work in *Movie Maniacs*.

Publicity photo for *False Alarms* (1936), posed elegantly by Larry, Moe and Curly.

I remember the fantastic gooey mayhem during the making of *Hoi Polloi* in 1935. I stood off-camera with a cream puff in each hand. Our leading lady, Grace Goodall, was at the end of a long dining room table in a very elegant dining room. The scene called for her to laugh loudly with her mouth wide open. Director Del Lord, who did many of our films in those days, asked me to throw one cream puff directly into her face while she was laughing. The butler would stand behind her, say the word *disgusting,* and turn around, and I was to hit him square on the back of the neck with the other cream puff.

Del shouted, "Action," and the scene proceeded normally. On cue, I let fly with the first cream puff and hit Grace squarely in the mouth. The butler said his line and I let fly with the other, scoring a bulls-eye right in the back of his neck. When Del called, "Cut," we found our leading lady with the cream puff lodged so deeply in her throat that she was gasping for breath. Some of the cream had gone down her windpipe. We did have a moment of concern until we brought her around.

I happened to catch *Slippery Silks* on TV recently and I distinctly remember that in this sixteen-minute comedy more than 150 pies were thrown. I had a sore throwing arm for almost two weeks and a pretty sore face. The ones I didn't toss were thrown at me.

Moe convinces Larry to take the next alarm that is rung in *False Alarms*.

The zanies indulge in a spot of relaxation between fires in *False Alarms*.

The boys return to a less complicated time, in the company of Beatrice Blynn and Elaine Waters, in *Whoops, I'm an Indian* (1936).

The boys test the equipment in *Half-Shot Shooters* (1936).

Curly, Moe and Larry drool over their next meal in *Slippery Silks* (1936).

The Stooges' *Slippery Silks* nemesis is, as usual, Vernon Dent.

In 1937's *Goofs and Saddles,* Curly is Wild Bill Hiccup and Moe plays Just Plain Bill.

A real emergency arose during the course of shooting. We ran out of pies! The property man rushed in and swept up all the whipped cream he could collect from the floor. In the dirty cream were dust, nails, and splinters. He added a little marshmallow sauce and, with some leftover crusts, whipped up a batch of new pies. When these gooey missiles hit us in the face with nails inside, the results were almost disastrous. Sometimes the old saying that "The show must go on" can be carried a bit too far.

Being on the receiving end of tossed pies was fraught with problems. Sometimes it was impossible to wipe the mess out of your eyes so that you could get back your vision and continue the scene. As rough a character as I seemed to be in pictures, and as tough as I came across, I was hurt in our films more often than either Larry or Curly or any other member of the cast.

In the comedy *Beer and Pretzels,* we played carpenters. I was on top of a table measuring shelves and shouting the dimensions down to Curly. He bent over, and placed a board on the table I was standing on, and proceeded to cut it to the proper dimensions with a circular saw until he cut right through the table. As I turned around to get the board from him, the table broke in half and I fell. I knew how to break my fall but there was no avoiding the fallen table. The side of my body landed on the upright legs. I had five words to speak, which I did, and then passed out. Hours later at the hospital, I learned I had three broken ribs.

I remember once when the prop man concocted a smorgasbord of gook: chocolate, whipped cream, asbestos chips, linseed oil, ketchup, and other unknown goodies. I was supposed to fall face down in a vat of something or other with Curly dropping right on top of me. As luck would have it, I forgot to close my eyes. Curly had me buried under that goo for about eight seconds. When I came up, nostrils and eyes full of that brutal concoction, they needed the studio doctor and a nurse to bring me back to normal . . . something I haven't been for years.

Oily to Bed and Oily to Rise, another 1939 goodie, was—what else—an oil well picture. The plot had us in one scene, trying to repair a water pump. After many attempts, I took a screwdriver,

95

In trouble out West in *Goofs and Saddles:* Larry, Moe and (temporarily) Curly.

Frontiersman Howard, Howard and Fine in *Back to the Woods* (1937).

Moe, Larry and Curly take time out in 1937 to menace Moe's daughter, Joan.

Fellow Columbia actors Melvyn Douglas, Virginia Bruce and Margaret Lindsay demonstrate Three Stooges hand puppets (1937).

Larry, Curly and Moe stumble upon the cache in *Cash and Carry* (1937).

The boys always are available for a bit of tutoring, and in *Cash and Carry,* young Sonny Bupp is the recipient of their expertise.

Moe, Curly and Larry are less than impressed as they examine their horse in *Playing the Ponies* (1937).

Larry and Moe discover the secret of getting Curly to smile in *The Sitter-Downers* (1937).

In *Wee Wee Monsieur* (1938), Harem girls Curly, Moe and Larry compare biceps with John Lester Johnson.

The Stooges clean up their act in *Three Missing Links* (1938).

Moe and Helen in 1938, celebrating another wedding anniversary.

Archeological nuts Larry, Curly and Moe in *We Want Our Mummy* (1938).

Moe, Larry and friend in *Three Missing Links*.

Moe, Curly and Larry break bread with some furry friends in
Calling All Curs (1939).

knelt down, peered into the mouth of the pump, and jiggled the screwdriver inside of it. Gazing up the opening, I jiggled again and then looked up a third time. Suddenly a blob of assorted gunk got me right in the eye again. And again it took hours to clean me up for the next scene.

In another film we were playing the parts of women. I was wearing the usual high-heeled shoes and, in skipping out of the room, one heel turned under me. I slid to one side and, not wanting to fall in the scene and ruin the shot, I dove out into the next room, hit my head on the leg of a bed, and was knocked cold. The next day I was on crutches with a fractured ankle.

Curly also had his share of injuries. I remember a short where Curly was playing both himself and his father. There was one sequence where he was to be pushed down an elevator shaft, which was really just a hole dug in the floor deep enough for Curly to drop completely out of sight. They padded the floor of the hole with mattresses but neglected to cover a nearby two-by-four. When Curly was pushed into the opening, his head hit the edge of the two-by-four, cutting his scalp wide open. We pulled him out and made him comfortable until the studio doctor arrived. He looked at the wound, washed it off, put some colodion on it, then clipped the hair from around the wound. I stood by watching in amazement as the doctor glued fresh hair into the bald spot and Curly continued with the scene.

Then there was the time Larry got it. We were dentists in a scene where some plaster was being thrown around. The property men got a little too enthusiastic, and they cracked Larry in the eye with a good-sized chunk of plaster. In another short, he had a tooth knocked out, and once he got stabbed in the forehead with a quill pen.

But we were Stooges, and that was what we were getting paid for, getting what little brains we had knocked out. Hi-diddle-dee-dee . . . an actor's life for me!

Off the Movie Set for a While and On to Broadway

IT WAS 1935 and my daughter Joan was nearly eight years old. Bookings for personal appearances between shorts were constant, and when school was out, Joan always traveled with us. She enjoyed going to the zoos in the various cities. However, Helen and I came to the decision that it wasn't fair to Joan to be an only child, and although she was the love of my life I often dreamed about having a son—someone to take fishing and play ball with—so we planned for another child and Helen became pregnant. As the end of her term drew near, I was on the road. In order not to be too far away, Helen and Joan took the train from California to New York, where Helen could be near me and her sisters. I was appearing in Boston at the time. She went to Doctors' Hospital for the delivery, and I remember phoning her there: "Honey, if it's a boy, they'll have to drag me out of the gutter, I'll be so drunk."

The next day I received a wire. It read, "It's a boy, keep out of the gutter." My wildest dream had come true.

Curly, Larry, and I had been booked into the RKO Boston Theater and were at Grand Central Station in New York preparing to leave for Boston. I had promised to phone Rube Jackter, head of the sales department of Columbia, to let him know about doing a benefit performance in Boston for the Children's Hospital. I called to okay the performance and before we finished talking, he said, "Moe, the night editor of the New York *Times* would like to speak with you." I joked and said, "I hope it's not another benefit in Boston." A few seconds later, the *Times* man was on the phone, and without any greeting, aside from "Is that you, Moe?" he asked. "Would you like to make a statement on the death of Ted Healy?"

I will never be able to describe the terrible feeling in the pit of my stomach. Stunned, I dropped the receiver. I don't know how long I stayed in that phone booth, only that thirty years flashed into my mind along with the memories of my entire association with Ted. I did not know that the tears came to my eyes as I rested my head on my folded arms. Curly and Larry suddenly pushed the phone booth open and dragged me to the train.

I followed the boys, sobbing all the way, and I heard Larry telling Curly, "Your brother is nuts; he's actually crying." I didn't say anything to the boys until I got into our hotel suite in Boston—I just couldn't talk about it. I finally gave them the news that Ted was dead and that beyond that I knew nothing.

When we got back from Boston, I got the story. It seems that Ted was at the Trocadero, the famous nightclub on the Sunset Strip in Hollywood, drinking up a storm, when he got into an argument with three patrons. Ted called them every vile name in the book and then offered to go outside and take care of them, one at a time. The four men went outside and, before Ted had a chance to raise his fists, they jumped him, knocked him to the ground, and kicked him in the ribs and stomach. Ted's friend, Joe Frisco, a well-known comic, picked him up from the sidewalk and took him to his apartment. Ted passed away a few days later of a brain concussion. At the time of his death, his salary in the theater was $8,500 a week. There was no vaudeville star who earned more. He was also under contract to MGM at a very high salary. With all this, it's hard to believe that his friends had to give a benefit to pay for his burial. Brian Foy (of the Seven Little Foys) footed a great part of the funeral bill and helped pay off other debts Ted had incurred. What a sad ending! When sober, Ted was the essence of refinement; while under the influence, he became a foul-mouthed, vicious character. Liquor had killed his father and uncle and had destroyed his sister's life. When Ted was young, I remember that he made a pledge never to touch liquor, after having seen the consequences of its effects on his family. The strain of his life in show business got him started, and once he started drinking he was never able to stop.

At the end of July 1939, the Three Stooges were booked for two weeks at the Palladium in London. We made the trip over on the *Queen Mary,* a beautiful ship. Our reservations were for second-class passage, but we were moved up to first-class quarters by the captain, who had seen and enjoyed our comedies in England. The voyage was pretty rough and passengers were sitting on deck with buckets beside them.

Curly interrupts the boy's punch-spiking plans in *Three Sappy People* (1939).

My sea legs were pretty good, so the rough waters didn't bother me, but Larry wasn't taking the trip too well. I suggested that he stroll the deck for some fresh air. We had only walked a few feet when Larry heard one of the passengers retching. At the first sound, he took off for his cabin as though he were shot out of a cannon.

We arrived in London to an amusing double headline in the paper: "Stooges arrive in London—Queen leaves for America." Our first Palladium engagement was a success, and we were asked to stay on for a second. We also appeared in Blackpool, England, a summer resort, and then went on to Dublin, Ireland. We arrived in Dublin by taxi. The crowds were thick and the cars were thicker, and we suddenly found our taxi hemmed in. We couldn't move and found ourselves in the midst of a riot. Men were hanging from lamp posts with clubs in their hands and swinging at anyone within reach. The sidewalks were jammed with people swinging fists, clubs, and sticks. Bobbies, six feet tall, armed with billy clubs, swung them over the heads of the people. Every so often, a fist would come up from the crowd and hit a bobby smack in the face. We finally reached our destination and ran from the cab to the theater lobby. The manager of the theater told us that the Irish from Northern Ireland had many of their martyrs buried in the South and had started a march to

Moe and Curly during their Dublin stage appearance in 1939.

visit their graves. The bobbies had put a chalk line across the sidewalk and warned the leaders not to cross it. One of the leaders, a woman, waved a flag and beckoned her followers over the line, and then the riot started. The manager explained to us that something like this took place every year and resulted in hundreds of injuries. The gang from Northern Ireland never made it and were always driven back.

After this wild welcome to Dublin, we were greeted by the owner of the Royal Theater, a Jewish cantor with an Irish brogue so thick you could hack it with a cleaver. "Now, boyos," he told us, "I can't put the name, 'The Three Stooges,' on the marquee because in Dublin, here, when the boyos have an affair with a girl they call it 'stooging,' so you'll notice that I changed your names to the 'Three Hooges.'"

We did exceptionally well in Dublin, then went on to Glasgow for a week at the Empire Theater. On our way to our hotel, we were followed by a group of pink-cheeked youngsters. They locked arms with us and, before we knew what was happening, they had torn the patch pockets from our coats and run off with Curly's hat. They only wanted souvenirs. Three bobbies came to our rescue.

The Foster Agency, which had booked us in Great Britain, came to us in Glasgow with a batch of new contracts for thirty more provinces. We explained that we had signed to appear in the *George White Scandals of 1939* and had to be back in New York for rehearsals. It was late August and any other bookings would be impossible.

On our return to London, we found that bomb shelters were being built in Hyde Park and that fire drills were being held. It gave us a strange feeling to see all this going on, not realizing a war was imminent.

On the upper balcony of our hotel was a television set and we could see everything that was going on in Hyde Park and other parts of London. This was our first introduction to television.

Fortunately our passage back to the States had been booked on our arrival to London. As I recall, we left London in the middle of 1939, on the *Queen Mary*. It was the last civilian trip she made until after World War II.

In July 1939, we went into rehearsal for *George White's Scandals*. We were still under contract to Columbia but in our lay-off period between comedies. After breaking in in Boston, the *Scandals* opened on Broadway on August 28 and turned out to be a very successful show. The cast included Willie and Eugene Howard, Ben Blue, Ella Logan, The Stooges, and a young tap dancer named Ann Miller.

Matty Brooks and Eddie Davis wrote most of the comedy sketches; many are still done today. One famous sketch, "The Stand-In," had a pie-throwing sequence that was a pretty messy piece of business. After the first show in Atlantic City where we were breaking in the new material, George White himself came out with a push-broom and helped sweep up the mess. After the first show, this sketch was done on a large rubber mat so that the stagehands only had to pull it out and hose it off backstage.

I neglected to mention that Lois Andrews, not of the Andrews Sisters, was also in the show. She was quite attractive and George White really went for her. One day he pressed a little too hard and this sixteen-year-old girl tossed a right to George's jaw that knocked him through a mirrored door. Lois later married Georgie Jessel, who was three times her age.

During the run of the *Scandals,* a tremendous electronic sign had been built atop a building on Times Square. It consisted of thousands of flashing electric light bulbs which formed a pattern of the Three Stooges in silhouette, in action. Thousands of people would watch it as they walked along Broadway on their way to night spots and restaurants. And I must admit Helen and I admired it, too. I stood there in the street, lost among the crowd, and watched myself and the boys slapping each other and doing the eye-poking routine. I can remember standing among the laughing people and listening to their remarks. This is what I'd worked so hard for. Then I would go into the theater with my heart as light as a feather. This is a part of show business that I shall never forget.

Shortly before the *Scandals* ended its Broadway run, Larry, Curly, and I had to go back to the Coast to resume filming for Columbia.

Helen and Moe with Morton Downey's Coca-Cola tour.

Into the Forties

IN 1940 WE WERE SHOOTING A COMEDY called *A-Plumbing We Will Go,* with director Del Lord. We had filmed about ten pages of our twenty-nine-page script the first day and another ten by lunch time the next day. Then we all went to screen the dailies, or rushes, as they are called, where you see what you've shot the day before. During the screening we all noticed a shadow revolving in the lower part of the frame. It was continuous and remained there through the entire previous day's work. No one could figure out what it was or how it got there. Filming continued after lunch when, during one of the scenes, I noticed the director sitting in his usual spot just under the lenses of the camera. I also noticed that he had two fingers wrapped around a clump of hair and he was nervously twirling it around and around. We were in the middle of a take and I stopped dead in my tracks and called to him, "Del, I've solved the shadow problem." When I explained to him that his hair-twirling habit was being filmed along with our comedy, he was dumbfounded. It cost the studio seven thousand dollars to reshoot the film to get rid of the mysterious shadow.

There was one director with whom we worked who shall, for obvious reasons, remain anonymous. He was a nice chap but he had one problem: he liked girls and he had no trouble amassing quite a collection. He would meet a girl and promise her a part in a picture. It was a great line. This finally became a problem because these girls, although very attractive, had one failing: they couldn't act.

Plumbing as taught by Curly in
A-Plumbing We Will Go (1940).

A trio of little darlings capture, in *Nutty But Nice* (1940),
the appreciative glances of Vernon Dent and John Tyrrell

In *You Nazty Spy* (1940), the boys have raised the
ire of Don Beddoe, Richard Fiske and Dick Curtis.

In vaudeville, again in 1940, with Eddie Laughton their white-suited foil.

Vernon Dent once more is on the receiving end of the Stooges' pranks in *Dutiful But Dumb* (1941).

The Stooges' plot to take over the world is foiled by Little Billy in *You Nazty Spy*.

The Stooges do a vaudeville turn with Florine Dickson in *You Nazty Spy*.

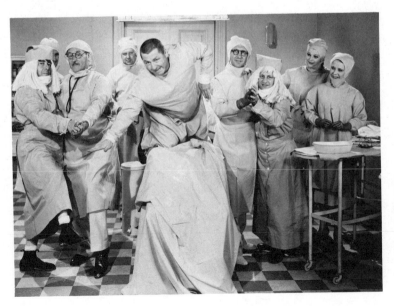

In *From Nurse to Worse* (1940) the boys take a dance break in the operating room. Moe teams up with Vernon Dent and Larry with John Tyrrell, while Curly amuses Dorothy Appleby and Babe Kane with a smart buck-and-wing.

Larry, Moe and Curly stroll to a 1940 vaudeville date between films.

Our director would spend hours on the set getting a passable performance from them until the producers would complain and ask why the films were going over schedule. He'd throw the blame to us, telling them that the Stooges just couldn't remember their lines.

When I recall the broad spectrum of the vaudeville dates I've played, I think of the worst times and the best times—they stand out so vividly. My blackface act with Shemp, where we were the clean-up act, had to be the worst of vaudeville, and a tour which we made with Morton Downey and his band for the Coca-Cola Company was by far the best from the standpoint of sheer luxury.

The Coca-Cola Company footed the bill and we played every army, navy, and air force installation from Maine to Pensacola. We did—dream of dreams—one show a night, and before each one, we were the guests of the commanding officer and ate at the officers' club. After the show there was always a gourmet dinner given by the local Coca-Cola bottler.

We traveled in a private air-conditioned bus. My wife and Morton Downey's wife accompanied us. Reservations were made for us in the best hotels. Each morning we would start out in a happy mood. We'd climb aboard the bus, the band would play, we would read or relax on the way to the next town. This was one-nighter show business at its best.

The highlight of this tour turned out to be the naval base in Pensacola, Florida. When Admiral Price learned that Downey and the Stooges loved to fish, he set up an unforgettable trip. The day started with naval air maneuvers. We witnessed an amazing air drop of fourteen hundred parachutists. Then the admiral ordered a sleek, twin-screw ship to pick us up. Its larder was filled with sandwiches and beer on ice. The ship was equipped with a large bait container. It was fascinating to watch the ship's communication with a helicopter which flew overhead scouting out schools of fish for us. The twin-screw ship could slow down just enough for trolling. The admiral's aide had a drop line with some bait on it; when he got a bite, he'd wave to another seaman, who would drop anchor and put out a yellow marker. Then we all began to fish: Morton, the boys from his band, we Three Stooges, and Admiral Price, who believe it or not, was cutting bait for us.

Not to turn this into an unbelievable fish story, I ended up catching about eighty pounds of red snapper and twenty trigger fish.

Three Stooges in a tub that shows every sign of sinking in *A-Plumbing We Will Go*.

The boys clown with Franchot Tone on the set of their Columbia feature *Time Out for Rhythm* (1941), and Curly looks amazingly like Lou Costello as he flirts.

Despite the confines of their cell in *In the Sweet Pie and Pie* (1941), Eddie Laughton manages to remain spotless as the Stooges wield paint brushes.

Moe, Curly and Larry are in mythical Moronica doing another of their Hitler spoofs in *I'll Never Heil Again* (1941).

Challenging Duncan Renaldo, Don Barclay and Jack Lipson for control of the world in *I'll Never Heil Again*.

The Columbia "family" entertains some Navy brass in 1941. The Stooges kneel in front with Arthur ("Dagwood") Lake. Standing are a group of visitors surrounding Brian Aherne (with pipe), Rita Hayworth, Allyn Joslyn, Jinx Falkenberg, Wallis Clark, Evelyn Keyes, Glenn Ford, Claire Trevor, and Janet Blair.

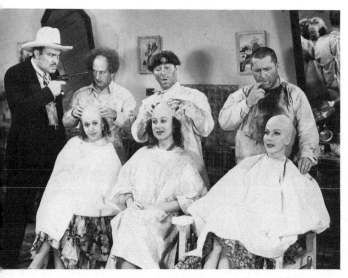

In *Loco Boy Makes Good* (1941), Larry, Moe and Curly are inept hairstylists, and although Bob O'Connor is leery of their technique, Dorothy Appleby (left) and her friends seem resigned to their fate.

The bull mugs with the boys before the ring action of *What's the Matador?* (1942).

Assigned to track down a missing gorilla in *Dizzy Detectives* (1943), the Stooges have trouble determining who are the good guys and who aren't.

The boys subdue the baddies, including Vernon Dent (officer at right), in *Back from the Front* (1943).

Larry, Curly and Moe give it to Adolph in *Higher Than a Kite* (1943), and even Jack Curtis is taken in.

The expected zaniness in *Dizzy Pilots* (1943), as the Stooges take a breather from their dedicated pursuit of inventing a new plane.

In *A Gem of a Jam* (1943), Larry and Moe have difficulty convincing Dudley Dickerson that the man in white is Curly

With Larry's assistance, Moe prepares to demonstrate his versatility with a sling-shot in *Phony Express* (1943).

The Stooges are on safari — with skis, golf clubs and snowshoes, as well as Monte Collins and Louise Carver in *Some More of Samoa* (1941).

Curly pulls one of his own teeth to put Moe's fear at ease in *I Can Hardly Wait* (1943).

Nancy Carroll drops by Columbia to examine one of Moe Howard's legendary hooked rugs.

Trying to do their wartime bit as farmers, the Stooges are confronted by rustic oldtimer Emmett Lynn in *The Yoke's on Me* (1944).

Curly mistakes a fishbowl for a water cooler in *A Gem of a Jam*, forcing Larry and Moe to come to the rescue.

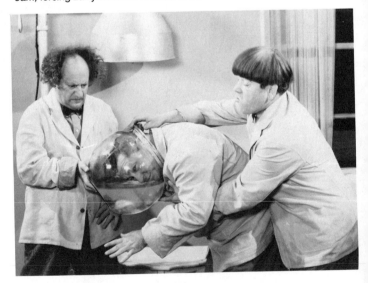

The boys take a few moments from
filming chores for publicity shots

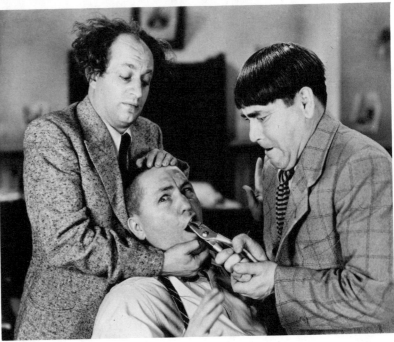

The boy's traditional disputes.

124

Domestic Wartime Interlude

DURING WORLD WAR II, we were all planting Victory Gardens. I had one of my own in a small patch of open space that once contained a rose garden in the back of my home in the Toluca Lake area of North Hollywood. I had purchased three building plots covered with walnut and apricot trees. Our architect also had built Bing Crosby's home nearby. We built on only half of the land and I held the other half for resale, using this portion for a potato patch until selling it to Raoul Walsh in 1945.

During construction, I was on tour (as usual) with Larry and Curly. I had returned early in 1940 to find our home completed. It was a charming English manor house—two stories, a three-car garage, swimming pool, badminton court, and formal gardens. Helen and I lived there with the kids until we sold the property in 1955.

Often in the summer, for the fifteen years we lived there, I would barbecue. I really enjoyed cooking, and sometimes it was for quite a mob. As far as swimming went, I dove into the pool about a dozen times in all those years, and that was to pick up the hairpins from the bottom so they wouldn't leave rust marks—shades of Annette Kellerman's divers. Our son, Paul, learned to swim in that pool and later became a letterman at UCLA in swimming and water polo. Joan later was married by that same pool, which we covered at the time with beautiful pond lilies. There wasn't a frog to be found on those lily pads.

In 1944, recalling the happy days on the farm in Chatham, I planted a victory garden on the vacant lot next door. All my friends and neighbors knew me as the gardener with the green thumb and the pot belly. I planted potatoes, onions, green peppers, corn, tomatoes, you name it—even parsley, sage, rosemary, and thyme.

While I waited for my crops to grow, I decided to raise chickens. I built two chicken houses to match the architecture of our home: hand-hewn shake roofs, hardwood floors, casement windows. I bought thirty silver-laced Wyandotte hens and two roosters. During this time, my brother Shemp asked me to build him a hen house, too. He would supply the material, and while I built his hen house, he went to a poultry farm and picked up a dozen hens. I found out later he had forgotten to buy a rooster.

Weeks had gone by and my garden was coming along fine. I was busy killing bugs, propping up the tomato plants, cultivating and weeding. I remember going through the furrows one day in the lettuce bed and finding about five heads were missing. There weren't any dead plants; just five holes in the ground. I couldn't figure it out until one early evening, I noticed one of the lettuce heads shaking as though it had the chills; then, before my eyes, that lettuce head disappeared into the ground. Now I knew that the gophers were having a vegetable feast. First, I set traps, then I ran

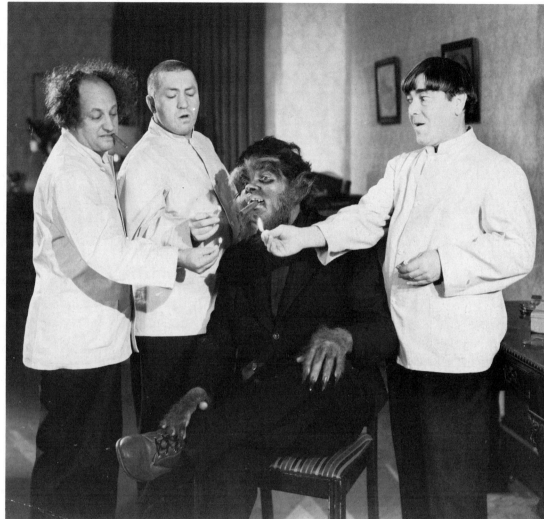

the garden hose into the gopher runs and only ended up washing out a good portion of my plants. My cat got a few and I sat by the hole, hour after hour, rifle in hand. Not only were gophers wiping out my garden, but some human animal was coming around and pulling up my potato plants, stealing my corn, beans, and onions. I even sat up all night waiting to catch the culprits, but all I came up with were a couple of neighborhood kids. One threw a rock and hit me in the head as I chased him. How did he know that I was prone to head injuries? Finally, I turned the case over to the police. I don't belive I got four meals out of that entire crop, but I certainly was kept busy.

By now the first batch of chickens that I was raising was ready for the pot. I bought a barrel and some heavy brown paper to line it—and a nice sharp meat cleaver. I then took the chickens out one at a time and tied them up. The first one I placed head down gently on the stump of a nearby apricot tree, raised the cleaver, turned my head away and came down hard with the blade. Without looking I threw the bird into the barrel, where I heard it flapping around in the bottom. It made me sick to my stomach. I turned to get away from the awful sound, and there at my feet lay the head with one eye winking at me as though it had approved of what I'd done. I dropped the cleaver and ran to the house. Our hired hand finished the job for me, but I was unable to eat my chickens or anyone else's for months afterward.

Moe hopes his Japanese disguise will help
him infiltrate a Nazi gang in *No Dough Boys*
(1944).

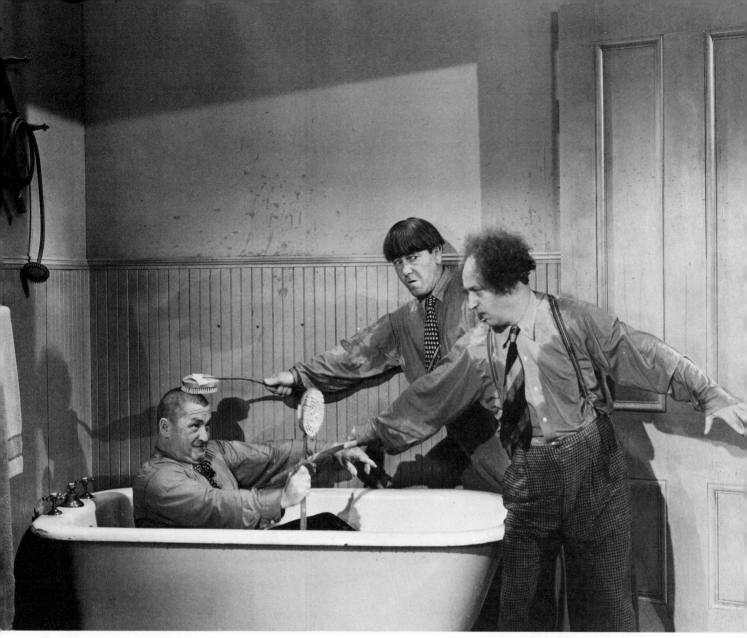

The zanies scrub up for their forthcoming
marriages in *Gents Without Cents* (1944).

During this same period, Shemp was having his poultry problems, too. His wife, Babe, came
to me one day and said, "Moe, Shemp's chicken, Veronica Lake [Her comb hung over her eye],
flew into the neighbor's yard and is digging up his plants. Please help us. He not only hates chickens, he hates everybody."

The next day, I rode over on my bicycle and found Shemp leaning over the fence with a thin
wire lasso in one hand a fistful of corn in the other. He was dropping the corn in the center of the
loop of the lasso, attempting to snare Veronica. Every time she grabbed the corn, Shemp would
miss snagging her. He finally gave up that method and turned to another one. He baited a fish hook
with a worm, cast it over the fence, trying to hook Veronica like a fish. But she would bite the end
of the worm off and run away leaving the other half still on the hook and Shemp holding the bag.
After a while the score was Veronica, 12—Shemp, 0.

"Take it away, Shemp," I said, "there's only one way to catch her." I took a handful of corn
and climbed the fence, with one eye open for Shemp's mean neighbor. I laid a trail of seed to a

The boys' wedding trip in *Gents Without Cents.* The gals, left to right, are Lindsay Bourquin, Betty Phares and Laverne Thompson.

Moe relaxes at home with son Paul in 1944.

In *Gents Without Cents,* the Stooges
play vaudevillians in benefit shows for the
war effort, and even here are given the hook:
Curly, Betty Phares, Larry, Lindsay
Bourquin, Moe, Laverne Thompson.

small mound of corn, and when Veronica got to the corn, I grabbed her by the neck and shot back over the fence with her. I gave her back to Shemp, who punched Veronica in the eye and threw her headlong into the hen house. Early the next morning, he went to the local butcher and traded his twelve live hens for six dead pullets. He held Veronica until last and gave her one last affectionate whack in the eye before handing her over to the butcher. So ended our farming and chicken business.

During the war, Helen and I entertained soldiers in our home. I went through air raid drills as an air raid warden but, unlike our wild comedies, I didn't foul up—at least, not too much.

I can still remember an afternoon when things really hit home. We heard a crash in the rear of our garden just a few feet from the pool. An army training plane had smashed into the telephone wires and hurtled to the ground, killing the pilot.

Toward war's end, my daughter fell in love with a sailor, Norman Maurer, a photographer stationed at the Long Beach navy base. He was a comic book cartoonist and a very handsome and likable fellow. After a two-year courtship, they were married. The wedding took place in our garden: water lilies in the pool, the tennis court covered with a wooden dance floor, the garden spilling over with flowers. Where none could ever grow, the florist just inserted them. The ceremony was

One disaster-prone hunting trip is forthcoming in *Idiots Deluxe* (1945), with idiots Moe, Curly and Larry.

followed by a lavish dinner served at umbrella-covered tables while two orchestras added the final touch.

It was not long before I spotted, in Norman's work as a comic book cartoonist, a close parallel to the movie industry. He wrote the stories and dialogue, directed his characters, cast them, created their wardrobe, etc. Years later, when we finally did our features for Columbia, Norman was assigned the job of writing and producing them, and he directed our last two features.

Joan and Norman gave us two grandchildren, Michael and Jeffrey. Number three is my son Paul's daughter, Jennifer. One day, I recall, Joan phoned me and asked if I wouldn't pick up her boys after school. Always being the early bird, I parked my car and decided to wait in front of the school. A short time later Mike and Jeff came charging out, followed by about two hundred screaming kids stampeding toward me. It looked like a Merrill Lynch commercial. The boys had told their friends Moe was picking them up. Friends had told friends, and the word of mouth created a minor mob scene. It wasn't long before an indignant teacher rushed up to me and told me that I'd better leave—I was inciting a riot.

Another time, I received an urgent message at the studio to call Joan immediately. Fearing the worst, chicken Moe phoned her to learn that Michael and Jeffrey had found our picture in one of the volumes of the World Book Encyclopedia which she had just bought for them.

Stooges in an encyclopedia! I didn't believe it! She was pulling my leg. That night, I found out. There in Volume C, under the heading *Comedy*, was a single illustration: a photograph of Larry and me bending a crow bar around Curly's neck.

Under the heading of trials and tribulations was a weekend show date we had booked. Curly had just bought a beautiful new car. We were working in Hartford during the week and were headed for Willamantic, Connecticut, for a midwinter weekend. The snow was heavy and, as we left Hartford, it had started to rain. The roads were soon covered with a thin layer of ice to go with deep

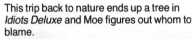

This trip back to nature ends up a tree in *Idiots Deluxe* and Moe figures out whom to blame.

133

The Stooges, behind bars for bootlegging in
Beer Barrel Polecats (1946), indulge in their
usual harrassment of warden Vernon Dent.

Southern gents Larry and Moe are annoyed
at the attention Curly is getting from Marilyn
Johnson, Eleanor Counts and Faye Williams
in *Uncivil Warriors* (1946).

Monkey Businessmen (1946) finds the goofy
trio in a shady sanitarium.

banks of snow along the edges. Curly was driving and, after approximately fifteen miles, the country roads became quite hilly. On one steep incline, Curly's car started sliding from one side of the road to the other and finally went completely out of control. We began skidding in tight circles despite the fact that Curly was doing a masterful job of trying to control the car. A few terrifying moments later, it started careening backward for what seemed an eternity and suddenly smacked into a snowdrift and came to a stop. Larry and I got out, congratulating Curly on his fantastic steering.

Surveying the situation, we wondered what would be the best way to proceed. Curly kept revving the motor and twisting the steering wheel, but the rear wheels just kept spinning and shooting out a geyser of ice and snow. We put the jack under one of the rear wheels, but the spinning wheels just buried the jack deep into the snow. Finally, I came up with a sensational idea. I reminded the boys that we had our stage wardrobe in the trunk. I placed two stage coats and one pair of pants under one wheel, and a dressing room robe and two makeup towels under the other one, and then told Curly to get in the car, start the motor and give it gas. Never in my life did I ever see such a shower of clothes flung in every direction. We never did find our wardrobe. A farmer finally got us out of our difficulty by selling us a half bale of hay and tossing it under each wheel. We made it to the theater fifteen minutes before show time and found we were the only act, out of five, that got there. We did an entire one-hour-twenty-eight-minute show without leaving the stage. The audience went wild.

One Sunday afternoon I was barbecuing chicken for twenty-four guests. I had picked up fourteen nice-sized broilers at the Farmer's Market, cleaned them and cut them in half, and

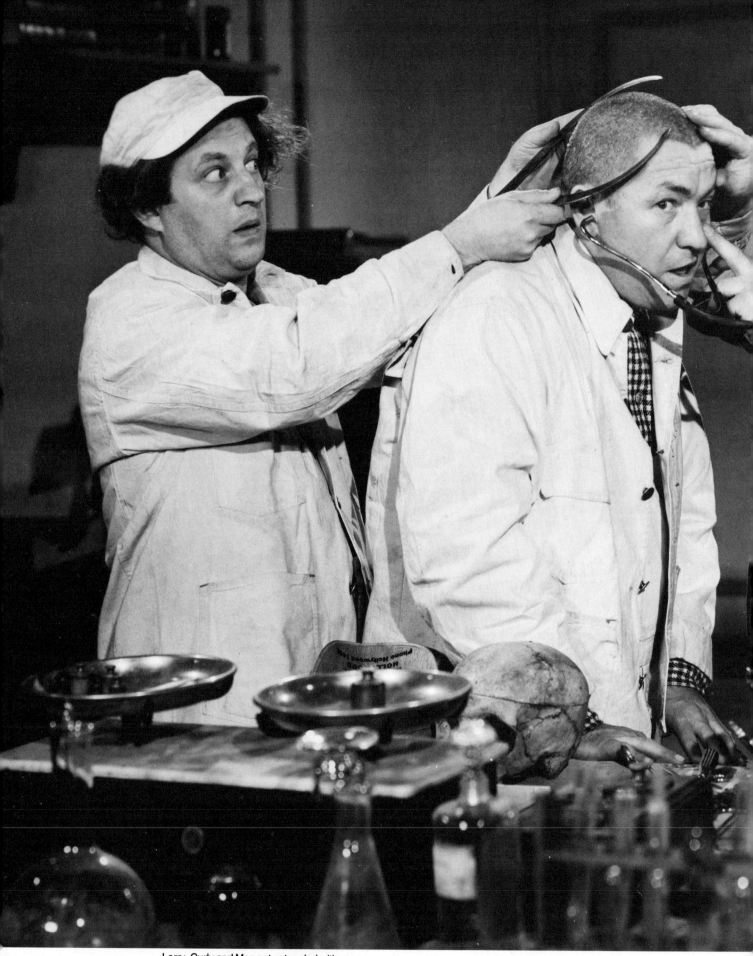

Larry, Curly and Moe get entangled with
mad scientist Vernon Dent in *A Bird in the
Head* (1946), and it's Curly's brain he wants.

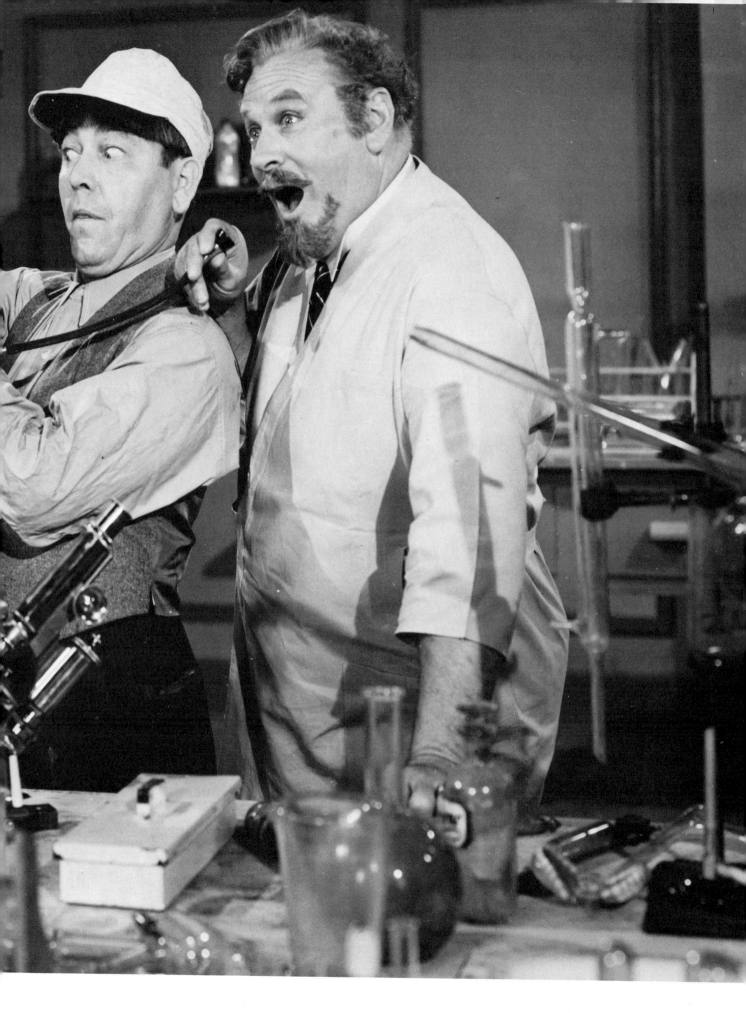

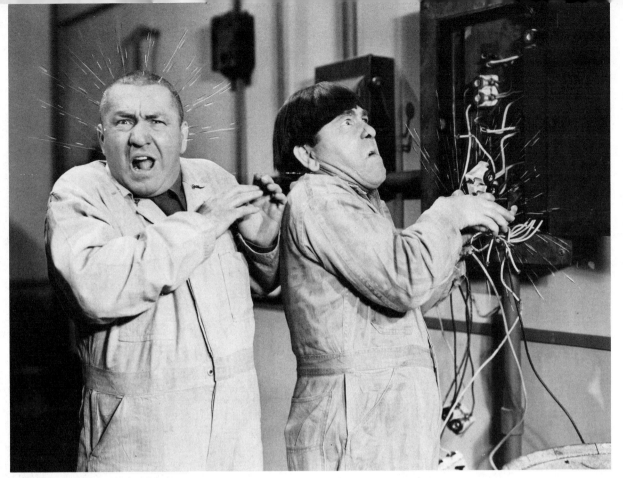

Curly is genuinely shocked at the way Moe
changes a blown fuse in *Monkey
Businessmen*.

Larry, Curly and Moe are ex-GI's in *G.I.
Wanna Go Home* (1946), eager for their first
stateside meal.

In *G.I. Wanna Go Home* the boys are dragged to the altar by Judy Malcolm, Etheldreda Leopold and Doris Houck.

brushed them with my special sauce. I put them in the refrigerator to marinate for a few hours. I was going to cook these twenty-eight chicken halves on my barbecue and another one that I had borrowed from a neighbor.

At about one in the afternoon, I was ready to put the birds on the fire made with hickory charcoal and wet hickory shavings, which I lit with an electric starter. I laid out the chicken halves on the two barbecues. It was a seemingly endless task. First I brushed and turned and basted the chicken on one barbecue, then I brushed and turned and basted the chicken on the other. What a chore! It took me over an hour, but at last they were done to a turn—and so was I. All that basting and rotating had me dizzy.

Well, the meal was great; that was the consensus of all my guests. I was all in! That night I had a nightmare in Technicolor.

Larry, Moe and Curly are obliged to fill in for a trio of girls who failed to show up in *Rhythm and Weep* (1946).

I remember vividly seeing myself basting those chickens turning from barbecue to barbecue, when suddenly, while my back was turned, one of the chickens flew off the portable barbecue and made about four turns in the air above my head. It was totally naked; no feathers at all. Smoke was streaming from its fanny. It made one more fast circle in the air and then flew through the door that opened from our living room to the porch where I was barbecueing. Now flames were shooting out of its behind. I chased it into the living room, wielding my barbecue fork and taking swipes at it as it flew around the room, shooting flames like a flame thrower. I kept missing it. It flew behind our drapes. I was frantic. Now the drapes were smoking and burning. I couldn't get to any water to put the fire out so I took the only course of action possible. I opened my fly and shot a stream of urine at the drapes. At that moment, I felt a blow on top of my head. This wasn't a dream. My wife was yelling, "What are you doing. I'm soaked . . . you've wet me . . . and why are you yelling, 'Fire, fire'?" I was never so embarrassed in my life. After that night, I vowed never to barbecue for more than my family.

Moe is father of the bride at daughter Joan's 1947 wedding to Norman Maurer. Young Paul is part of the bridal party.

Changes Among the Stooges

DURING OUR LAYOFF period at Columbia in the mid-forties, we were contracted by the owners of a small, rather rundown theater in New Orleans who wanted us to play on their bill. They turned out to be the Minskys of burlesque fame. Harold Minsky, who was a true showman, was attempting to change over a small house to vaudeville and wanted to get name acts that would draw customers. His mother and father were operating the theater while Harold took care of booking the acts.

Ludicrous as the situation may seem, the elder Minskys had not been on speaking terms for many years. If Mrs. Minsky wanted to say something to her husband, she would do it through Harold: "Tell that idiot to stay in the department, where he belongs." Then Mr. Minsky would reply through Harold, "Tell Mrs. Idiot to mind her own part of the business." As if Harold didn't have enough to worry about, he had Mr. and Mrs. Minsky.

Minsky's theater was set up so that at the back of the last row of seats a section was set aside for standing room, where about eighty people could be tightly wedged together. There was an exit door at each end of this section, with a crash bar across the door in case of fire or other trouble. In the front of the theater were six steps the width of the front, which was about sixty feet wide. Flanking the steps were guard rails; to the right was the box office where Mrs. Minsky sold her tickets. Behind was another box office with a cashier who sold tickets to blacks only. Remember this was New Orleans, and black people could sit only in the gallery.

When Harold Minsky asked the Stooges to play his theater—I took care of the business for the act—I replied, "Our salary has gone up since the old days. We now get forty-five hundred a week."

Harold said, "I need you fellows very badly. What kind of a deal can you make me?"

I told him, "Harold, you guarantee us fifteen hundred dollars. We'll get four acts for you and

142

Shemp is back with the Stooges and gets a roaring welcome in *Hold That Lion* (1947).

Moe, as St. Peter, tells Shemp he can't enter the Pearly Gates until he reforms his fellow earthbound Stooges, as Marti Shelton takes notes in *Heavenly Daze* (1948).

Vagabond Loafers (1949) has Shemp doing the role Curly had played in an earlier version of the film (A-Plumbing We Will Go).

In Heavenly Daze, the boys demonstrate one of their utensils to a vaguely interested Victor Travers and Symona Boniface.

The boys take a break in their search for missing pearls in Hugs and Mugs (1950).

The Three Stooges as broads in Self-Made Maids (1950).

Shemp and Moe, in Dopey Dicks (1950), congratulate themselves on foiling the villain, although Stanley Price has a surprise for them.

Larry, Shemp and Moe display their ingenuity as census-takers in Don't Throw That Knife (1951).

The Stooges, director Edward Bernds and Hugh McCollum accept the 1951 Exhibitor's Award to Larry, Shemp and Moe.

In *Self-Made Maids,* Larry helps Moe put the finishing touches on his makeup.

you give us a fifty-fifty split from the first dollar above our fifteen hundred." Harold thanked me profusely for giving him a break. I then realized after making the deal that the only way we would do good business was to create a maximum amount of audience turnover. I found the answer to this problem after the first performance. I announced to the audience that if they would line up at the stage door in the alley next to the theater that we would give each person a picture. Although it was raining like mad outside, our loyal fans lined up just to be able to get an autographed photo. Meanwhile, the house had cleared and another group was packed in.

That was a week to remember. Mrs. Minsky sold tickets in the front box office, and I recall standing out front one day. A woman saw me and said to her friend, "That's the ugly one who hits the two nice Stooges." Her friend replied, "Don't talk like that. He just keeps the other two guys in line like my Albert does with our two boys." Mrs. Minsky's face beamed as the people kept pouring in: "Moe, I have a sneaky feeling that we're going to make a lot of money." Then, a large, swarthy woman stepped up to the box office and asked for two adult tickets and three juniors. The woman was carrying a child completely covered by a blanket. Mrs. Minsky reached out and uncovered the child who turned out to be a boy of fifteen—with a mustache yet. Mrs. M. was a tough old bird and at one point, when the theater was jammed, she kept urging the people to come in, saying that there was plenty of room inside. It was so packed that one man who was already inside was shoved to the outside by the crowd and was forced to buy another ticket to get in again.

That week we gave away a grand total of thirty thousand pictures and did fifteen-thousand dollars worth of business. This was fantastic for that size house. The Minskys wanted us back, but our contract kept us from returning.

It was May 14, 1946, a day so indelibly imprinted in my mind. We were just finishing *Half-Wits' Holiday*, a remake of one of our favorite comedies, *Hoi Polloi.* It was a clever, funny film that brought to an end the career of one of the great comics of his time.

Curly sat in director Jules White's chair waiting to be called to do the last scene of the day, while I was finishing one with Larry. It was terribly humid and the heat on the sound stage was stifl-

Daffy detectives Moe, Larry and Shemp again get themselves entangled in offers to solve a mystery in a haunted castle in *Scotched in Scotland* (1954).

The boys' adventures in a Scottish castle puts them close to Christine McIntyre, one of their frequent leading ladies, in *Scotched in Scotland.*

Hugh McCollum and Christine McIntyre pose with the Stooges in *Scotched in Scotland* before the boys embark on their de-haunting of the castle.

Inept restaurateurs Shemp, Moe and Larry tangle with gangsters Kenneth MacDonald and Frank Lackteen in *Of Cash and Hash* (1955).

ing. Larry and I finished our scene, and the assistant director called for Curly to come in to complete the final scene of the picture. Curly didn't answer. I went out to get him and found him with his head dropped to his chest. I said, "Babe"—I called him sometimes by his childhood nickname—Curly looked up at me and tried to speak; his mouth was distorted and speech would not come. Tears rolled down his cheeks, and soon there were tears running down mine. I thought my heart would break. I immediately knew that he had had a stroke. I put my arms around him and kissed his cheek and forehead. He squeezed my hand but couldn't say a word. I had the studio car take him home while I finished his scene. When Jules finally said, "That's it. Wrap it up," I ran to my car without taking off my makeup or wardrobe and drove to Curly's house.

After Curly's stroke, I arranged for him to be taken to the Motion Picture Country Home in Woodland Hills where he could get the best of care and therapy. I was with him almost constantly.

Later, when I had time to collect my thoughts, I had the feeling that this would be the end of the Three Stooges. Who could take Curly's place? He was a genius in his field, kind, considerate, and so carefree and humorous. He drank far too much liquor and I knew the reason why. After his gun accident as a teenager, he was in quite a bit of pain when he stood too long. The fact that he had to shave his head for the act was also a factor: he felt that he had no longer any appeal for the fair sex. So he drank to give himself the courage to approach any young lady that appealed to him.

Shemp tries to impress Moe in *Gypped in the Penthouse* (1955) under the disapproving glare of gold-digger Jean Willes.

In *Blunder Boys* (1955), our heroes are at war with the army and the surrender is unconditional.

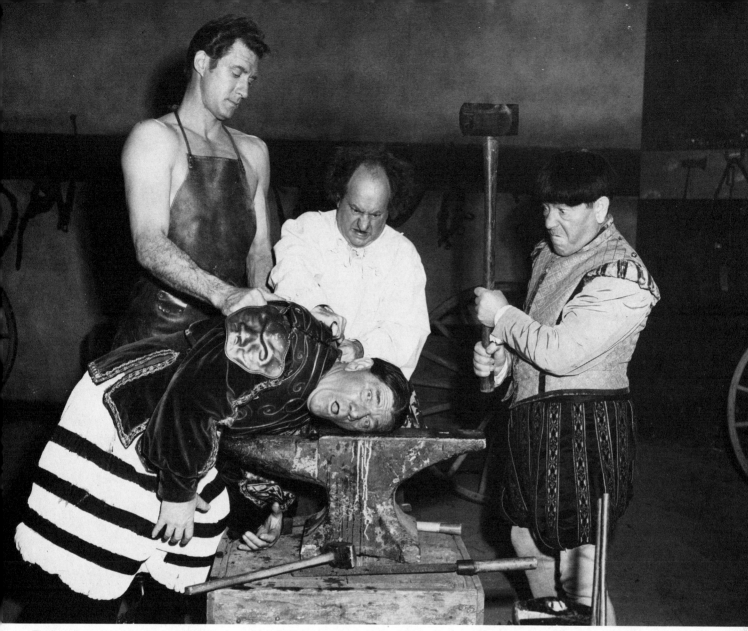

The boys borrow blacksmith Jock Mahoney's anvil for devious purposes in *Knutzy Knights* (1954).

Curly remained in ill health for six years, having additional strokes, and passed away in January 1952, at the age of forty-nine.

Larry and I wondered if it was possible to revive the Three Stooges. Many performers were presented to me by agents, but they didn't have a tenth of what was needed to fill the bill. Finally it hit me: why not Shemp! He had been one of the Stooges before Curly. I presented the idea to Columbia, but the front office felt that Shemp looked too much like me. So I told them it's Shemp or you don't have the Stooges anymore at Columbia. They quickly changed their minds, and Shemp once again joined the act. The Stooges were back in business again. I felt very low for a long time but never showed it. Every time I smacked or poked Shemp I was seeing Curly. This feeling finally left me and I was able to think clearly again.

The first two-reeler we did with Shemp back as one of the Stooges was *Fright Night,* in which we play fight managers. Ed Bernds directed that one. Later, when we made *Hold That Lion,* Curly came back to do a brief gag appearance. It was the only film in which all three of us Horwitz brothers appeared.

Philip Van Zandt and assorted baddies menace Moe, Larry and Shemp in *Knutzy Knights.*

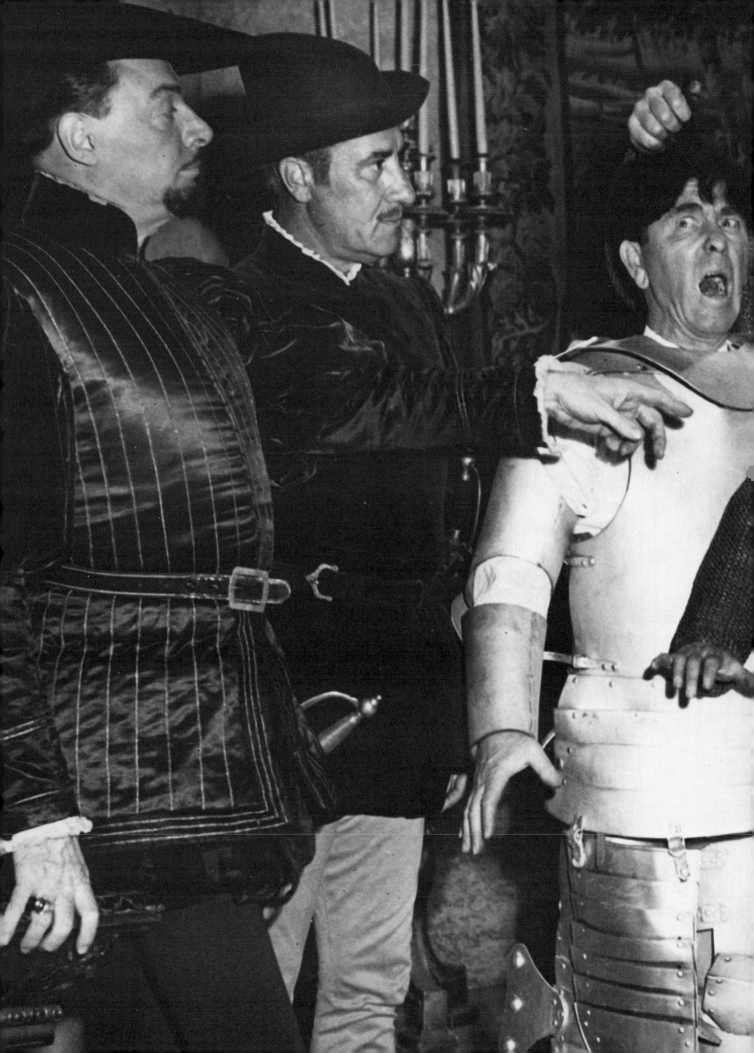

In 1955, Helen and I decided to sell our home in Toluca Lake and go on a cruise to Europe. Our stay abroad lasted about four months. These were happy days but my happiness was short-lived.

November 23 started as an ordinary day. Shemp had gone to the horse races in the afternoon and to the prize fights that night. All of Shemp's friends got a kick out of his reactions to the fights. He would jab, jerk, and duck in his seat reacting to the fighters in the ring. The audience would watch him as much as they watched the fight. People sitting on either side of him would often get up and change their seats to avoid jabs in the ribs from Shemp's wild blows. After the fights, Shemp got into the car of one of his friends, and was telling jokes when he suddenly dropped his head, leaned against one of the men, closed his eyes, and, with a smile on his face, died.

When I heard the news that night, I was dumbfounded. I had such a feeling of loneliness and frustration. It took me weeks to gather my thoughts, to make plans for the future, and to try once more to put the act together again. I don't know what I would have done without Helen's encouragement, for at that moment I wanted to give it all up.

Helen and Larry urged me to go on with the act, and I slowly brought myself around to finding a replacement. I started out by trying to get Joe DeRita to take Shemp's place. I knew Joe's work from burlesque. He was fat and chubby with a round, jovial face, and, with his hair clipped close, he would look a great deal like my brother Curly. I went to see him and put the proposition to him. He told me he'd like nothing better than to get out of burlesque and join the Stooges. "But Harold Minsky has me under contract." No matter how much Larry and I pleaded with Minsky, he would not turn Joe loose. I could readily see why. Joe was the best comic he had. Now what to do?

I then recalled that Joe Besser, another chubby burlesque comic, had made several pictures at Columbia on his own and was known to television viewers for his stooging on Milton Berle's

The boys survey an escape route in *Pies and Guys* (1958) while unfriendly Milton Frome counts to three.

The boys try to convince their sister-turned-pony that she won't go to the glue factory in *Horsing Around* (1957).

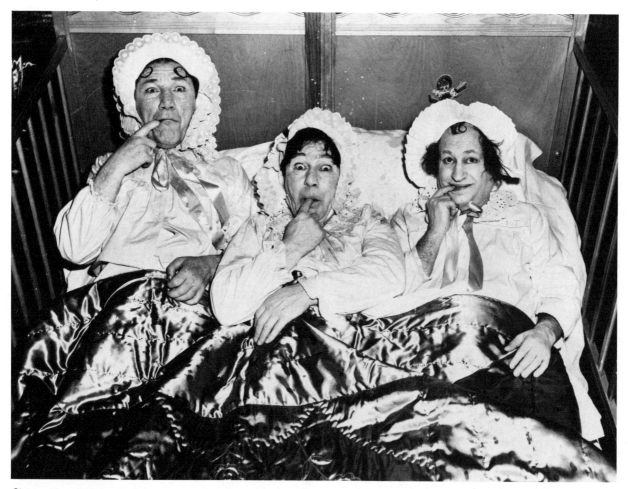

Shemp, Moe and Larry play their own sons in *Creeps* (1956).

Joe Besser's flair as a chef dismays Moe and Larry and their dates, Ruth Godfrey White, Jeanne Carmen and Harriette Tarler in *A Merry Mix-Up.*

Larry, Joe Besser and Moe confuse even themselves as identical triplets in *A Merry Mix-Up* (1957).

show. He, too, said that he would love to join the act except that he owed Columbia another two-reel comedy on his contract, but I talked the studio into releasing Joe from the deal and letting him join the Stooges.

The first short with the "new" Three Stooges was *Hoofs and Goofs*, in which our "sister" —played by Harriette Tarler—is reincarnated as a horse. In 1958, after making sixteen more two-reelers with Joe Besser, all directed by Jules White, we completed our contract with Columbia. Now what? Joe informed us that he could not go on tour with us, since his wife was ailing. Once again, a crisis in the Stooges' careers.

Here we were with an act that still had the potential to earn us a living—if not in films, then in personal appearance tours—and even though it seemed hopeless, I just couldn't let this happen. I had put so much into it through the years. Where to turn? What to do? I remembered Minsky had Joe DeRita. It couldn't hurt if I tried him again. To my surprise he said, "Moe, I'm in luck. My contract with Minsky is over next week, if you still want me." I said, "Joe, you're in. We'll start rehearsing with you next Monday."

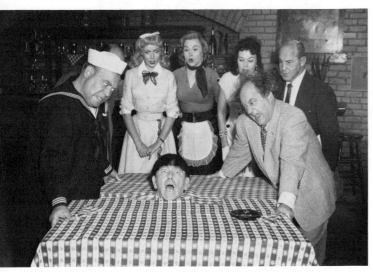

Moe blows his top in *Fifi Blows Her Top* (1958), as Joe and Larry try to keep him contained and Vanda Dupre, Harriette Tarler, Diana Darrin and Joe Palma look on.

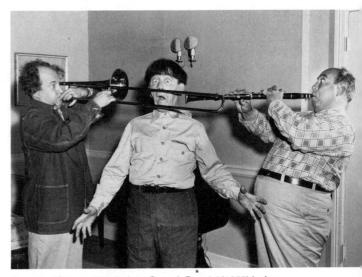

A musical Stooges interlude in *Guns A-Poppin'* (1957) before the boys depart for a cabin in the woods.

Joe Besser ends his stint as one of The Three Stooges with panache in *Sappy Bullfighters* (1959), the final Stooge short for Columbia.

Moe and Larry bid farewell to Joe Besser.

The Comeback
Larry, Moe, and Curly Joe

WE GOT BACK INTO ACTION in 1958 after finally getting Joe DeRita to join us, and we broke in our new act with a date at the Holiday Inn in Bakersfield, California. It was really a heartbreaker. Business was lousy and the audience, a flock of beer-drinking sheepherders, was unreceptive. They didn't understand our humor. We got two laughs: one when I poked Joe DeRita—Curly Joe, as we called him—in the eyes, the other when I hit him in the stomach. One man kept putting liquor in his beer and, after a few minutes, began yelling at us, "Quiet, you're waking my friend up!" I leaned over and said, "You now have thirty-two teeth; would you like to try for none?"

I was terribly discouraged, but I tried not to show it. How we got through that show I'll never know. At the second one, we switched our material and got a few laughs. There were two more days, which meant four more shows in all. I wasn't sure I could make it. I longed for Curly or Shemp. If it weren't for the fact that my wife was beside me, I might have broken down completely. I was ready to quit the whole thing. I told myself this must be a bad dream or maybe this was what I needed to spur me on to a greater effort.

The next night, the club owner even tried to renege on his contract with us, complaining about bad business. He asked us to take a substantial salary cut. My son-in-law, Norman Maurer, convinced us to turn him down. If the club's business had tripled, we would not have been entitled to another dime, so if receipts were slimmer than anticipated, we shouldn't have to give any refunds.

At our next performance after the argument, my heart was pounding terribly. Out on the stage we went, all smiles, the actor's mask which frequently covers heartbreak. We kept switching

155

Curly-Joe DeRita becomes the third Stooge in style in 1959.

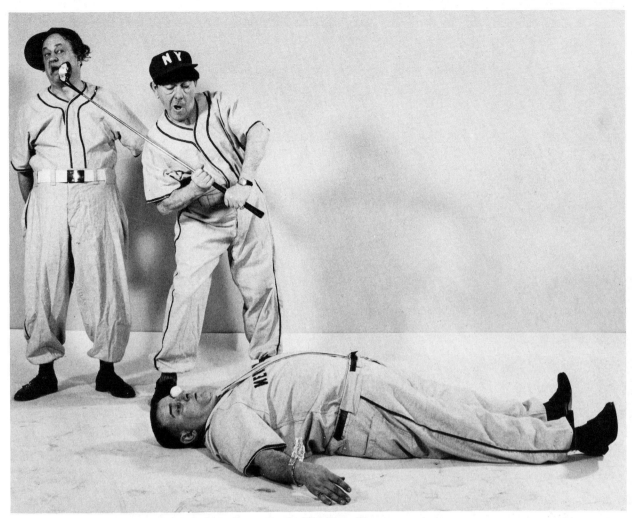

Clowning for a *Life* magazine spread on the fantastic comeback of The Three Stooges.

material, even sticking in a few off-color jokes. The patrons' reception of us improved slightly, we were getting some solid laughs, but it was a far cry from the old days.

Night clubs, I decided, just weren't for us. Our film career was over; we were really meant for vaudeville, but vaudeville was dead.

I wondered where our next booking would be.

Then we learned through the grapevine and trade-paper articles that Columbia Pictures, through Screen Gems, its TV subsidiary, was putting together the first batch of thirty or forty Three Stooges shorts for television. The bulk of them were old, dating back to the 1930s, and Columbia did not hold out too much hope for their success, offering the package at bargain prices. Almost overnight, the Three Stooges became one of the hottest children's TV properties. A whole generation—millions of kids who had never seen the Three Stooges—were suddenly exposed to something brand new in TV fare. Popeye cartoons had been dominating the TV market kids found that we were *live* characters who did the wild, exaggerated antics of animated characters, and did them even wilder. Variety headlined an article about the new Three Stooges phenomenon: "Three Stooges As Screen Gems Top Bananas" and within a matter of weeks, the old Stooges shorts were the Number 1 children's TV series throughout the country.

The zanies have landed on a new planet and discover a peculiar-looking unicorn in their first film after being "rediscovered," Columbia's *Have Rocket, Will Travel* (1959).

It's mayhem as usual as Moe and Larry try to dig their way back into their rocket in *Have Rocket, Will Travel*.

Frances Langford, rehearsing her TV special in 1960, refuses to be intimidated by the Stooges.

Word of our new success spread fast in show business and offers started to pour in from every part of the country. The Stooges were back in business with a flood of offers for records, comic books, fairs, shopping center promotions, movies, TV, and so on. Suddenly, the entire nation seemed to have gone Stooge-crazy, and we were in a position to command salaries ten and twenty times what we had been getting. That Bakersfield club appearance had brought us $2,500 for the week. Now we were being offered as much as $25,000 a day to dedicate a new shopping center in New York.

In the summer of 1958, John Bertera, the owner of a Pittsburgh night club and restaurant, was reading the Sunday paper. His three young children were lying on the floor near him, watching television and laughing hilariously. The father looked up from his paper and said, "Now come on, kids, stop all that racket, you're disturbing me."

"We can't help it," the older boy said, "these guys are terrific." Bertera got up to watch the show and found himself joining their laughter. He asked, "Do you like those fellows so much?" and his son replied, "Dad, the whole school is crazy about them."

About one week later Bertera's agent contacted us and asked if we wanted to play the Holiday House in Pittsburgh for five days. I saw no harm in it—the money was good—so I okayed the date. We arrived in Pittsburgh on a Monday, did a couple of TV appearances on station WTAE with Paul Shannon, who was the host of our comedies on that station.

We opened on the following Thursday and we did smash business for the whole week. Bertera's agent asked us to come back and do an additional three weeks with a substantial raise in salary and an option for two more weeks. We did something at Holiday House that we had never done before in our act: we made our entrance through the audience, packed with kids. It felt strange with all these children reaching out, just wanting to be able to touch us.

Larry, Moe and Curly-Joe tip-toe their way into your heart on the Frances Langford television special.

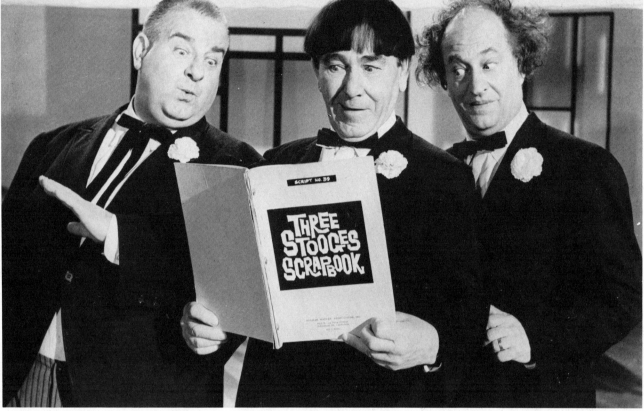

Publicity for the boys' retrospective of earlier Stooges shorts for Columbia's feature film, *Three Stooges Scrapbook* (1960).

At the end of the three weeks, John Bertera picked up our option for the other two, at another raise in salary. During the weeks that followed, Paul Shannon held a contest on TV, awarding prizes to the youngsters sending in the best likeness of the Stooges done in the most unusual way. We were staying at the Holiday Inn and, during the week of the contest, we received twelve large mail bags containing letters and packages by the thousands—we estimated about 25,000 pieces. We had to take an extra room to hold all of it. I remember how one ten-year-old winner painted our likenesses on three hard-boiled eggs.

At the close of our engagement, Bertera told us that it was the first time in the twelve years he had been operating the club that children had brought their parents.

He said to me, "Moe, this may not interest you, but we have started on our third ton of hamburgers, and it is very strange but if it weren't that my kids were crazy about you fellows, I would never have booked you."

Moe, Larry and Curly-Joe sense danger ahead and try to warn Edson "Prince Charming" Stroll and Carol Heiss in *Snow White and the Three Stooges* (1961).

Passing themselves off as medicine men in *Snow White and the Three Stooges,* the boys advertise as "Ye Stooges Three, Sole Purveyors of Yuk."

We did three Ed Sullivan shows. Now Ed was a very nice man, but for a showman, quite forgetful. On our first appearance, he introduced us as the Three Ritz Brothers. He got out of it by adding, "who look more like the Three Stooges to me." We also did three shows for Steve Allen. In one we did our stand-in sketch from the George White Scandals. I came close that night to missing the only performance of my career, but I went on despite a temperature of 103°. After the show, I went to bed for over a week. It's hard to believe that in sixty years of performing I had never missed a single performance. Clean living—and lots of good luck.

We did TV with Ed Wynn, Kate Smith, Frances Langford, Merv Griffin, and Joey Bishop. Our one show with Milton Berle wasn't very enjoyable. With all due respect to Milton's talent, I guess I'm spoiled. I don't like being on the receiving end of slapstick. Especially since Berle came across with a slap in one routine which cracked my front tooth.

Finally, after all these years of waiting and pleading with Columbia to make a feature, they came to us with an offer to make one, called *Have Rocket, Will Travel*, with my agent Harry Romm

Larry, Carol Heiss, Curly-Joe and Moe freeze it up in *Snow White and the Three Stooges.*

Larry, Moe and Curly-Joe appear to be taken in by villainous Guy Rolfe in *Snow White and the Three Stooges*.

Moe is visited on the set of *Snow White and the Three Stooges* by Joan and Helen and his grandson, Jeff Maurer.

On a publicity tour for *Snow White and the Three Stooges*, the boys join Spyros Skouras and his wife

producing. The film—our first feature-length movie in eight years—was released in 1959 and was a smash. It had cost less than $400,000 to make and brought in several million dollars to Columbia. By this time, we had made many personal appearances all over the country and had our own fan club with over 100,000 members. Photographs of the Stooges were on millions of Fleer Bubblegum trading cards; Western Publishing had put out a series of Three Stooges comic books; and there were Three Stooges toys, punching bags, puzzles, coloring books, puppets—to name just some of the countless items that appeared with our names and likenesses throughout the world.

In the latter part of 1958, we were signed by Twentieth Century–Fox to do a big-budget production—in Technicolor and CinemaScope. It would be called *Snow White and the Three Stooges*. Frank Tashlin would direct it and Snow White would be played by figure-skating champion Carol Heiss. The budget was set at $750,000. Instead of our standard deal ($50,000 and 50 percent of the net profits), we decided to waive our percentage and took $75,000 up front. Then Walter Lang, who had worked with us in the thirties on *Meet the Baron* at MGM and later did such major films as *State Fair* and *Can Can* and got an Academy Award nomination for *The King and I*, replaced Frank Tashlin, and Spyros Skouras gave him carte blanche on *Snow White and the Three Stooges*. Under Lang, the film's budget skyrocketed to $3,000,000. We Stooges never had been in such an expensive film. Luckily, we had gone for a straight salary, because our next picture, *The Three Stooges Meet Hercules*—made on a very small budget compared to the Fox movie—far outgrossed *Snow White*, which barely earned back its advertising and print costs.

With the box-office success of *Have Rocket*, Columbia immediately made us an offer to do a second picture with Harry Romm. At this time, however, we formed our own company, Normandy Productions, with Norman Maurer as our writer and producer (and sometimes director), and had decided that we wanted to do *The Three Stooges Meet Hercules* (the Hercules movies were big hits at the time) as our next picture. So we turned down Columbia's offer to do the second feature with Harry Romm and proceeded to prepare Norman's script for *Hercules*. For the first time in a quarter of a century, Columbia had made an offer to do a Stooge film and could not get the Stooges to go along with them. Unable to get our services, Columbia decided to make a Stooge feature without the Stooges and had Harry Romm piece together excerpts from our old shorts and edit them together into a film called *Stop, Look, and Laugh* with ventriloquist Paul Winchell as host. Seeing

Curly-Joe, Larry and Moe gang up to take on beefy Sampson Burke in *The Three Stooges Meet Hercules* (1962).

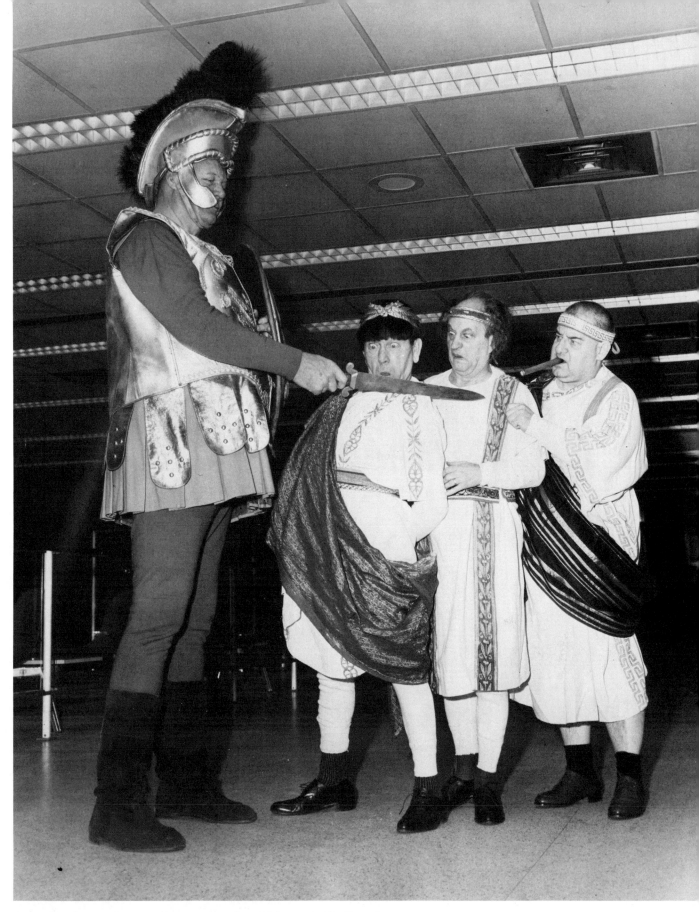

An imposing figure accompanies the zany trio on the publicity tour for *The Three Stooges Meet Hercules*.

In *The Three Stooges Meet Hercules*, the boys ogle a rather demure Vicki Trickett.

Moe and Helen at son Paul's wedding in 1961.

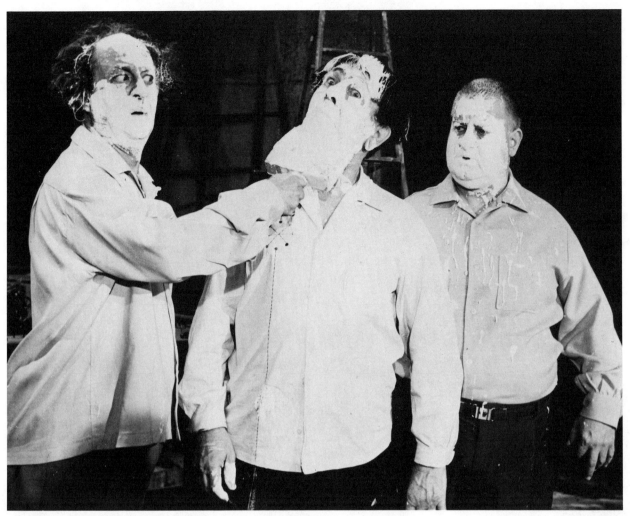

It's make up time for *The Three Stooges in Orbit* (1962), and Moe takes his turn getting plastered.

this as unfair competition, we immediately checked with our attorneys, who took the matter to the Superior Court of Los Angeles. We were issued an injunction preventing Columbia from releasing the film. Columbia apologized, admitted they were wrong, and agreed to a settlement whereby they would be allowed to distribute *Stop, Look and Laugh,* and would finance Normandy Productions' *The Three Stooges Meet Hercules.* Columbia also agreed never again to put together a Stooges feature utilizing old film clips without our permission. *The Three Stooges Meet Hercules* was released in 1962 and was an even bigger success than *Have Rocket, Will Travel.*

We went on tour with *Hercules,* and everywhere, rain or shine, lines stretched around the block. In San Francisco, I remember, the lines were beyond belief, beginning at the box office and ending less than five feet away. This may sound like a short line, but it actually went around all four sides of a city block and reached almost back to the box office.

When we got to New York with the film, we were staying at the Hampshire House on Central Park South. A strategy meeting was called during our stay, requiring all Three Stooges to be present. I phoned Curly Joe in his room and told him I'd pick him up there and then we'd both go to Larry's room. When I got to Joe's room, the door swung open and there he stood—stark naked, from the top of his shaven head to the tip of his clipped toenails. With his hairless body and roly-poly weight, it was difficult at first to tell whether he was a man or a woman. To my amazement, he stepped into the hall and insisted on having the conference right there.

Martians Og and Zog are genuinely baffled by Curly-Joe, Larry and Moe in *The Three Stooges in Orbit.*

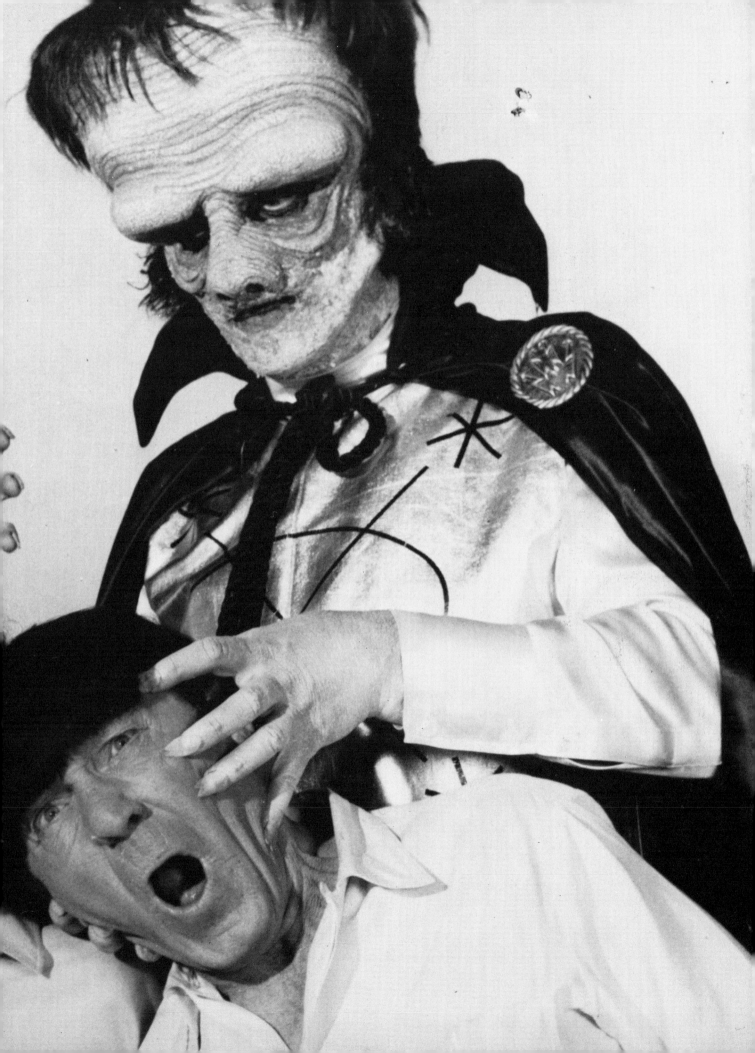

The Stooges contemplate a model of the tank/helicopter/submarine which will take them into space in *The Three Stooges in Orbit*.

In their get-up as extraterrestrial creatures, the boys stun Emil Sitka in *The Three Stooges in Orbit*.

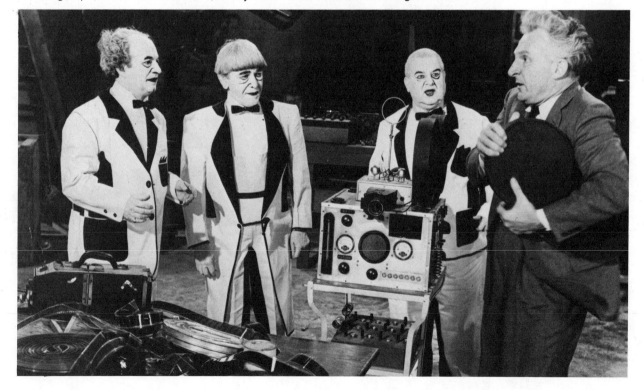

The success of *Hercules* was so great that Columbia gave Normandy Productions the go-ahead to do three additional features: *The Three Stooges in Orbit, Around the World in a Daze,* and *The Outlaws Is Coming,* which contained a love story between Nancy Kovack and Adam ("Batman") West. Norman directed the last two. We Stooges also made appearances in *Four For Texas* with Frank Sinatra and Dean Martin, and turned up as inept firemen in Stanley Kramer's *It's a Mad, Mad, Mad, Mad World.* After completing *The Outlaws Is Coming,* we made a deal with Heritage Productions in 1965 to do a series of animated color cartoons, called *The New Three Stooges.* Some 156 five-minute cartoons were produced for TV and are still in release.

In early 1971, we decided to do a TV series on our own based on an idea we had toyed with for several years: a series of color travel films with the Stooges visiting and fouling up the entire world. The title would be *Kook's Tour,* and it was designed to be a tour by three kooks. With a boat and camper, Larry, Joe DeRita, Norman (our producer-director), and I, plus our co-star, Moose, a black Labrador retriever, led a caravan of cars supplied to us by the Chrysler Corporation. We were driving through the Northwest seeking location spots for filming of the pilot for the proposed new series. It was a fresh and thrilling experience, shooting a film out in the fresh air in beautiful virgin country rather than the stuffy, confined stages to which we had become accustomed. When loca-

The Three Stooges are Ed Sullivan's guests on his Sunday night TV show.

The boys are packed for their newest adventure, *The Three Stooges Go Around the World in a Daze* (1963).

Romantic leads Joan Freeman and Jay Sheffield remain hesitant despite the backing of Larry, Curly-Joe and Moe in *The Three Stooges Go Around the World in a Daze*.

Taking *The Three Stooges Go Around the World in a Daze* to various openings throughout the country, Moe, Curly-Joe and Larry stop off to clown in Nashville, Tennessee.

Larry, Curly-Joe and Moe masquerade as Arabian sheiks in *The Three Stooges Go Around the World in a Daze.*

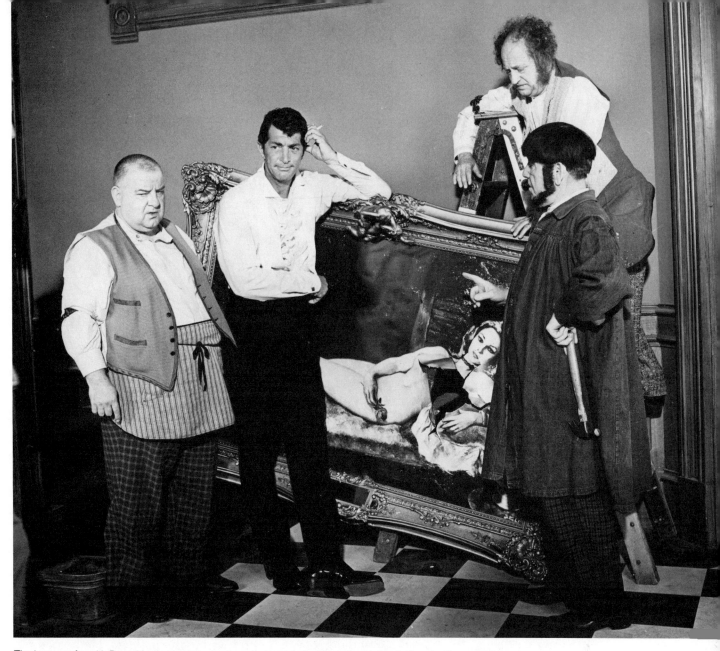

The boys confer with Dean Martin about the best way to hang Anita Ekberg's painting in *Four for Texas* (1964).

tion filming was completed, we headed back to Los Angeles to shoot closeups in the Angelus National Forest several miles from the city.

Then it happened. Larry had gone to his daughter's home to pick up clothing for the next day's shooting. That evening she telephoned me. Larry had had a stroke.

After weeks in the hospital, Larry attempted to recuperate at his daughter's home, but he needed daily therapy and wasn't getting it. I suggested that she have him placed in the Motion Picture Country Home Hospital in Woodland Hills, one of the finest institutions of its kind in the country. Every performing member of the film industry gave one percent of his weekly salary to maintain this institution. Funds also came from producers and directors (and occasionally, the public). At the home one received the best medical attention and care free of charge.

On one of my first visits to see Larry, I found he was beginning to look better, although his mouth was still affected by paralysis and his speech was very thick. I looked at him; he smiled a

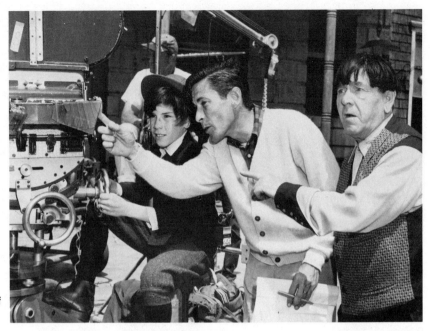

On the set of his last Stooges movie, *The Outlaws IS Coming* (1965), Moe and director Norman Maurer entertain Moe's grandson, Jeff Maurer.

crooked smile. I excused myself, saying I had to go to the lavatory where I broke down completely. When I managed to regain composure, I walked back into the room wiping my eyes. I told Larry I had just used my eye drops which made my eyes burn and tear. I had to get out of his room before I broke down in front of him. I explained that I had a doctor's appointment myself and that I would see him the following Sunday. I visited him almost every weekend after that and would push his wheelchair around while he played shuffleboard with the other patients. He enjoyed that very much.

After Larry's stroke, I knew the Three Stooges had come to an end as an act. Joe DeRita requested, and received, permission to do personal appearances with an act called "The New Three Stooges" with character actor Paul "Mousie" Garner and acrobatic comedian Frank Mitchell (who was half of the famous 1930s team of Mitchell and Durant). The act, unfortunately, never clicked and was booked into only a few engagements.

During his stay at the home, Larry did his best in entertaining the patients. He helped put on skits for their annual Ding-a-Ling Show. The entire cast performed in wheelchairs and would sing and move their chairs into chorus positions. I did a sketch or two with Larry at each performance. He became very adept at drawing, painting, and mosaic work, even though one hand was partially paralyzed.

Every visit to him became more trying. He would tell me jokes which were very hard to understand because of the thickness of his speech (my hearing problems didn't help), but I would yock loudly to cover the tears welling in my eyes. Over a period of months I could see that Larry was slowly getting worse. He always joked with me. I would laugh uproariously with tears falling at the same time.

Then, in late 1974, I phoned the home one day and was informed that Larry had been placed in the intensive care unit in the hospital. I tried to reach him there and was told he was unable to speak on the phone.

Shortly after the beginning of the New Year, I received another phone call from Larry's daughter. She said that Larry had become comatose and that little hope was extended by his doctors. A week later I received the call that really shattered me. Larry was dead.

The Stooges display annoyance that their boss, Sheriff Adam West, would take time out for some romance with Nancy Kovack while villains are loose in *The Outlaws IS Coming.*

Adam West is leery about the enthusiasm of his newly-sworn in deputies, Curly-Joe, Moe and Larry in *The Outlaws IS Coming.*

All's well that ends well in *The Outlaws IS Coming* as the boys wrap up their screen careers and Nancy Kovack heads for new horizons with Adam West.

The Stooges' new career: the animated New Three Stooges Cartoon TV Series (1965).

Larry and Moe clown on the New Three Stooges Cartoon TV Series, which included some live action.

Moe's son-in-law, Norman Maurer rehearses the boys for a special short promoting U. S. Savings Bonds in 1968.

The Stooges make one final film appearance on behalf of Uncle Sam in 1968.

Curly-Joe, Moe and Larry on the set of the abortive *Kook's Tour* (1970) with Norman Maurer.

The Stooges on their anti-pollution Vacuucycle in *Kook's Tour*.

A Single in the Seventies and My Seventies

AFTER LARRY HAD his stroke I really felt that the time had finally come for retirement, as far as being a Stooge was concerned. I signed up with an agent on the chance that there might be some character roles available, but I guess the producers were afraid that the Stooge in me might show through.

Then a letter came asking if I would appear at Salem College in West Virginia. It seemed that the nostalgia craze, where the Stooges were concerned, had hit hard. I went only because it was an excuse to go east and visit my son. I didn't know what I would do, though. How does one lecture at a university? I felt if I asked the students what they wanted to know about the Stooges, there would be bedlam with everyone yelling their questions at once. I decided that I would just talk briefly and express my pleasure at their wonderful reception. I told them, "I know what you fellows want to know about us, so I'm going to give you the answers before you ask the questions." I went through, in detail, all that I thought they would like to know. The idea went over well. I showed two of our comedies and told them a series of anecdotes, and they were delighted.

It was in September that I was asked to appear at the State Universty of New York at Buffalo. This time I had the audience fill out questions on cards and I would answer them from the stage.

The college auditorium was jammed. It had a 1,600-seat capacity and there were about 400 standing. The performance was broadcast on closed-circuit TV to all parts of the campus.

I remember that they showed a couple of our two-reel comedies, and then I did our whole

Moe Howard does a single in a 1972 personal appearance.

Moe and his older brother, Jack, a retired insurance salesman, discuss the possibility of reviving the Stooges.

Moe clowns with Helen and singer Sergio Franchi in 1973.

Never one to let a good pie go to waste, Moe takes up a familiar pose in 1973.

The last Moe Howard film appearance: Cinerama's *Doctor Death* (1973), with Sivi Aberg.

vaudeville routine doing Curly and Larry's part, too. During the question-and-answer period, one of the cards read: "Would you do me the honor of throwing a pie at me?" A young fellow came up on stage with his pie. Instead of the light whipped cream or shaving cream pies that we throw, this was the real thing, heavy with fruit and backed with a tin liner (ours were always backed with light weight cardboard). I frowned and explained the problem, but the young fellow wouldn't be deterred. I threw, the pie exploded, and the young man fell back a good five feet. He came up all smiles, and he thanked me.

I must say here that never in my career in show business, with or without the other Stooges, have I ever enjoyed such a standing ovation.

I'd come a long way from Moses Horwitz, high school dropout, to Moe Howard, Stooge, at New York University.

I continued on the college circuit, and occasionally on the TV talk shows in and around Los Angeles.

Helen and Moe in 1974.

For years I had envied the famous film scene where James Cagney smashed a grapefruit into his sweetheart's face. Finally, in 1974, my chance came. I was on national television doing a guest shot on the Mike Douglas Show. At the tail end of the show after an especially gooey pie fight, almost everyone was covered with whipped cream. I wound up holding the only remaining pie. I walked off the stage and into the audience where my wife, Helen, was sitting in the front row. The cameras followed me. I put my face affectionately close to hers, she leaned foward and I kissed her. Then, pie in hand, I walked back a few steps toward the stage, turned and slammed the pie into the face of Soupy Sales, who was co-host for that week.

Several months later I did the third Mike Douglas show and this time we again wound up in a pie fight and again I had possession of the last pie. Again I walked toward my wife in the front row and pie in hand, stuck my face out for a kiss. She leaned towards me with a pleased grin but instead of the kiss, she got the pie smashed right into her surprised face. The look was worth a million dollars. She began laughing and on national TV she kissed me, smearing my face with her—and my—pie.

When I performed on a fourth Mike Douglas show, Mike asked me to bring Helen up on stage to sit with him. I walked downstage and extended my hand to help my wife up. As I leaned over, she reached down for a concealed cream pie and slammed it right in my face, really clobbering me. A bull's-eye with the first pie she'd ever thrown—and one of the high points of our long life together.

AFTERWORD

MOE HOWARD continued on the college lecture circuit through 1974. He continued to appear occasionally on television with Mike Douglas, and he made one return to film acting—as a single this time—in a small role in a 1973 horror movie called *Doctor Death, Seeker of Souls*. He then began work on his autobiographical memoirs and was busy taping and transcribing at the time of his death.

After more than half a century of making people laugh, Moe Howard died on May 4, 1975, bringing down the curtain on one of the screen's legendary comedy acts.

Moe Howard in the mid-1970s

A Stooges Filmography

(Director's name follows title)
*2-reel musical

Ted Healy and His Stooges

Soup to Nuts (Fox, 1930) Benjamin Stoloff
Turn Back the Clock (MGM, 1933) Edgar Selwyn
* Beer and Pretzels (MGM, 1933)
* Hello Pop (MGM, 1933)
Meet the Baron (MGM, 1933) Walter Lang
Plane Nuts (MGM, 1933) Jack Cummings
Dancing Lady (MGM) Robert Z. Leonard
Fugitive Lovers (MGM, 1934) Richard Boleslavski
Hollywood Party (MGM, 1934) Richard Boleslavski
* The Big Idea (MGM, 1934)

Ted Healy, Larry, Moe and Shemp in *Soup to Nuts*.

196

In *Wee Wee Monsieur.*

The Three Stooges (Larry, Curly and Moe)

(Unless otherwise noted, all 16—18 minute two-reelers for Columbia)

Woman Haters (1934) Archie Gottler
Punch Drunks (1934) Lou Breslow
Men in Black (1934) Raymond McCarey
The Captain Hates the Sea (1934) (feature) Lewis Mile-
  stone
Three Little Pigskins (1934) Raymond McCarey
Horses Collars (1935) Clyde Buckman
Restless Knights (1935) Charles Lamont
Pop Goes the Easel (1935) Del Lord
Uncivil Warriors (1935) Del Lord
Pardon My Scotch (1935) Del Lord
Hoi Polloi (1935) Del Lord
Three Little Beers (1935) Del Lord
Ants in the Pantry (1936) Preston Black

Movie Maniacs (1936) Del Lord
Half-Shot Shooters (1936) Preston Black
Disorder in the Court (1936) Preston Black
A Pain in the Pullman (1936) Preston Black
False Alarms (1936) Del Lord
Whoops I'm an Indian (1936) Del Lord
Slippery Silks (1936) Preston Black
Grips, Grunts, and Groans (1937) Preston Black
Dizzy Doctors (1937) Del Lord
Three Dumb Clucks (1937) Del Lord
Back to the Woods (1937) Preston Black
Goofs and Saddles (1937) Del Lord
Cash and Carry (1937) Del Lord
Playing the Ponies (1937) Charles Lamont

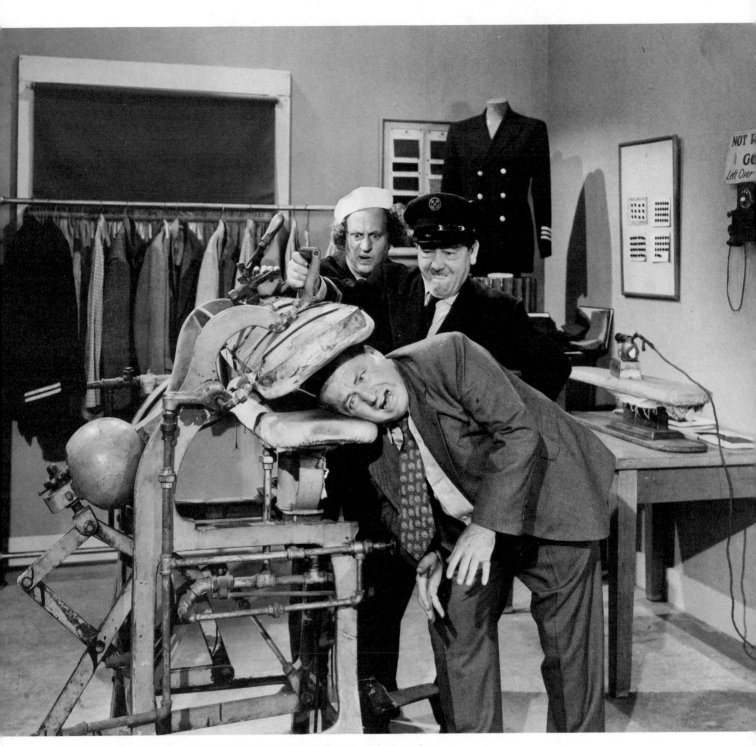

As Larry watches, Moe handles a pressing problem in *Three Little Sew and Sews*.

The Sitter-Downers (1937) Del Lord
Start Cheering (1937) (feature) Albert S. Rogell
Termites of 1938 (1938) Del Lord
Wee Wee Monsieur (1938) Del Lord
Tassels in the Air (1938) Charley Chase
Flat Foot Stooges (1938) Charley Chase
Healthy, Wealthy, and Dumb (1938) Del Lord
Violent is the Word for Curly (1938) Charley Chase
Three Missing Links (1938) Jules White
Mutts to You (1938) Charley Chase
Three Little Sew and Sews (1939) Del Lord
We Want Our Mummy (1939) Del Lord
A-Ducking They Did Go (1939) Del Lord
Yes, We Have No Bonanza (1939) Del Lord
Saved by the Belle (1939) Charley Chase
Calling All Curs (1939) Jules White
Oily to Bed, Oily to Rise (1939) Jules White
Three Sappy People (1939) Jules White
You Nazty Spy (1940) Jules White
Rockin' Through the Rockies (1940) Jules White
A-Plumbing We Will Go (1940) Del Lord
Nutty But Nice (1940) Jules White
How High Is Up? (1940) Del Lord
From Nurse to Worse (1940) Jules White
No Census, No Feeling (1940) Jules White
Cuckoo Cavaliers (1940) Jules White
Boobs in Arms (1940) Jules White
So Long, Mr. Chumps (1941) Jules White
Dutiful But Dumb (1941) Del Lord
All the World's a Stooge (1941) Del Lord
I'll Never Heil Again (1941) Jules White
Time Out for Rhythm (1941) (feature) Sidney Salkow
An Ache in Every Stake (1941) Del Lord
In the Sweet Pie and Pie (1941) Jules White
Some More of Samoa (1941) Del Lord
Loco Boy Makes Good (1942) Jules White
Cactus Makes Perfect (1942) Del Lord
What's the Matador? (1942) Jules White
Matri-Phony (1942) Harry Edwards
Three Smart Saps (1942) Jules White
Even as I.O.U. (1942) Del Lord
My Sister Eileen (1942) (feature) Alexander Hall
Sock-A-Bye Baby (1942) Jules White
They Stooge to Conga (1943) Del Lord
Dizzy Detectives (1943) Jules White
Back From the Front (1943) Jules White
Spook Louder (1943) Del Lord
Three Little Twerps (1943) Harry Edwards
Higher Than a Kite (1943) Del Lord
I Can Hardly Wait (1943) Jules White
Dizzy Pilots (1943) Jules White
Phony Express (1943) Del Lord
A Gem of a Jam (1943) Del Lord

The boys take a few moments from
filming chores for a publicity shot.

Larry Fine

Crash Goes the Hash (1944) Jules White
Busy Buddies (1944) Del Lord
The Yoke's on Me (1944) Jules White
Idle Roomers (1944) Del Lord
Gents Without Cents (1944) Jules White
No Dough, Boys (1944) Jules White
Three Pests in a Mess (1945) Del Lord
Booby Dupes (1945) Del Lord
Idiots Deluxe (1945) Jules White
Rockin' in the Rockies (1945) (feature) Vernon Keays
If a Body Meets a Body (1945) Jules White
Micro-Phonies (1945) Edward Bernds
Beer Barrel Polecats (1946) Jules White
Swing Parade of 1946 (1946) (feature for Monogram)
    Phil Karlson
A Bird in the Head (1946) Edward Bernds
Uncivil Warbirds (1946) Jules White
Three Troubledoers (1946) Edward Bernds
Monkey Businessmen (1946) Edward Bernds
Three Loan Wolves (1946) Jules White
G.I. Wanna Go Home (1946) Jules White
Rhythm and Weep (1946) Jules White
Three Little Pirates (1946) Edward Bernds
Half-Wits' Holiday (1947) Jules White
    (remake of Hoi Polloi)

Larry, Curly and Moe in *A Bird in the Head* (1946),

The Three Stooges (Larry, Shemp, and Moe)

Shemp Howard.

Fright Night (1947) Edward Bernds
Out West (1947) Edward Bernds
Hold That Lion (1947) Jules White
Brideless Groom (1947) Edward Bernds
Sing a Song of Six Pants (1947) Jules White
All Gummed Up (1947) Jules White
Shivering Sherlocks (1948) Del Lord
Pardon My Clutch (1948) Edward Bernds
Squareheads of the Round Table (1948) Edward Bernds
Fiddlers Three (1948) Jules White
Hot Scots (1948) Edward Bernds
Heavenly Daze (1948) Jules White
I'm a Monkey's Uncle (1948) Jules White
Mummy's Dummies (1948)) Edward Bernds
Crime on Their Hands (1948) Edward Bernds
The Ghost Talks (1949) Jules White
Who Done It? (1949) Edward Bernds
Hocus Pocus (1949) Jules White
Fuelin' Around (1949) Edward Bernds
Malice in the Palace (1949) Jules White
Vagabond Loafers (1949) Edward Bernds
    (remake of A-Plumbing We Will Go)
Dunked in the Deep (1949) Jules White
Punchy Cowpunchers (1950) Edward Bernds
Hugs and Mugs (1950) Jules White
Dopey Dicks (1950) Edward Bernds
Love at First Bite (1950) Jules White
Self-Made Maids (1950) Hugh McCollum
Three Hams on Rye (1950) Jules White
Studio Stoops (1950) Jules White
Slap-Happy Sleuths (1950) Hugh McCollum
A Snitch in Time (1950) Jules White
Three Arabian Nuts (1951) Edward Bernds
Baby Sitters' Jitters (1951 Jules White
Don't Throw That Knife (1951) Jules White
Scrambled Brains (1951) Jules White
Merry Mavericks (1951) Edward Bernds
The Tooth Will Out (1951) Edward Bernds
Gold Raiders (1951) (feature for United Artists)
    Edward Bernds
Hula La La (1951) Hugh McCollum
The Pest Man Wins (1951) Jules White
    (remake of Ants in the Pantry)
A Missed Fortune (1952) Jules White
    (remake of Healthy, Wealthy, and Dumb)

Listen, Judge (1952) Edward Bernds
Corny Casanovas (1952) Jules White
He Cooked His Goose (1952) Jules White
Gents in a Jam (1952) Edward Bernds
Three Dark Horses (1952) Jules White
Cuckoo on a Choo Choo (1952) Jules White
Up in Daisy's Penthouse (1953) Jules White
    (remake of Three Dumb Clucks)
Booty and the Beast (1953) Jules White
Loose Loot (1953) Jules White
Tricky Dicks (1953) Jules White
Spooks (1953) (in 3-D) Jules White
Pardon My Backfire (1953) (in 3-D) Jules White
Rip, Sew, and Stitch (1953) Jules White
Bubble Trouble 1953) Jules White
Goof on the Roof (1953) Jules White
Income Tax Sappy (1954) Jules White
Musty Musketeers (1954) Jules White
Pals and Gals (1954) Jules White
Knutzy Knights (1954) Jules White
    (remake of Squareheads of the Round Table)
Shot in the Frontier (1954) Jules White
Scotched in Scotland (1954) Jules White
    (remake of Hot Scots)
Fling in the Ring (1955) Jules White
    (remake of Fright Night)
Of Cash and Hash (1955) Jules White
Gypped in the Penthouse (1955) Jules White
Bedlam in Paradise (1955) Jules White
    (remake of Heavenly Daze)
Stone Age Romeos (1955) Jules White
    (remake of I'm a Monkey's Uncle)
Wham Bam Slam (1955) Jules White
Hot Ice (1955) Jules White
Blunder Boys (1955) Jules White
Husbands Beware (1956) Jules White
Creeps (1956) Jules White
Flagpole Jitters (1956) Jules White
    (remake of Hocus Pocus)
For Crimin' Out Loud (1956) Jules White
Rumpus in the Harem (1956) Jules White
Hot Stuff (1956) Jules White
Scheming Schemers (1956) Jules White
    (remake of Vagabond Loafers and A-Plumbing We
    Will Go)
Commotion on the Ocean (1956) Jules White

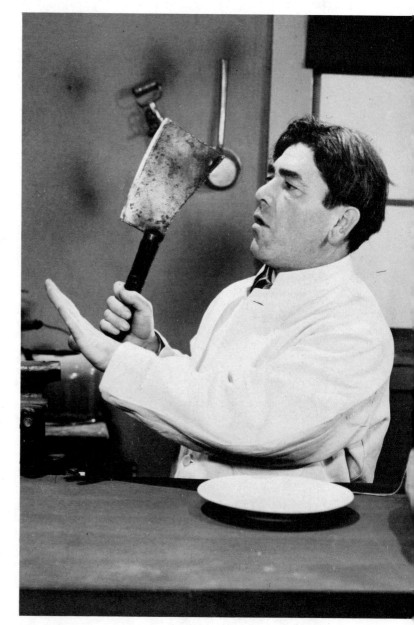

Moe Howard

Curly-Joe in *The Three Stooges Meet Hercules* (1962).

The Three Stooges
(Larry, Moe, and Joe Besser)

Hoof and Goofs (1957) Jules White
Muscle Up a Little Closer (1957) Jules White
A Merry Mix-Up (1957) Jules White
Space Ship Sappy (1957) Jules White
Guns A-Poppin' (1957) Jules White
Horsing Around (1957) Jules White
Rusty Romeos (1957) Jules White
   (remake of Corny Casanovas)
Outer Space Jitters (1957) Jules White
Quiz Whiz (1958) Jules White
Fifi Blows Her Top (1958) Jules White
Pies and Guys (1958) Jules White
   (remake of Half-Wits' Holiday)
Flying Saucer Daffy (1958) Jules White
Oil's Well That Ends Well (1958) Jules White
   (remake of Oily to Bed, Oily to Rise)
Triple Crossed (1958) Jules White
   (remake of He Cooked His Goose)
Sappy Bullfighters (1958) Jules White
   (remake of What's the Matador)

The Three Stooges
(Larry, Moe, and Curly Joe DeRita)

Have Rocket, Will Travel (1959) (feature) David Lowell Rich

Stop! Look! Laugh! (1960) (feature compilation of shorts) Jules White

Three Stooges Scrapbook (1960) (feature) Norman Maurer

Snow White and the Three Stooges (20th Century Fox, 1961) (feature) Walter Lang

The Three Stooges Meet Hercules (1962) (feature) Edward Bernds

The Three Stooges in Orbit (1962) (feature) Edward Bernds

The Three Stooges Go Around the World in a Daze (1963) (feature) Norman Maurer

It's a Mad, Mad, Mad, Mad World (United Artists, 1963) (feature) Stanley Kramer

Four for Texas (Warner Bros., 1964) (feature) Robert Aldrich

The Outlaws Is Coming (1965) (feature) Norman Maurer

The Stooges Alone:

MOE HOWARD
Space Master X-7 (1958) (feature for 20th Century-Fox)
    Edward Bernds
Don't Worry, We'll Think of a Title (1966) (feature for
    United Artists) Harmon Jones
Doctor Death, Seeker of Souls (1973) (feature for Cine-
    rama) Eddie Saeta
Senior Prom (1959) Associate Producer

SHEMP HOWARD
(As "Knobby Walsh" in Joe Palooka shorts for Vitaphone,
    1934-1937)
Headin' East (1938)
Hollywood Roundup (1938)
Millionaires in Prison (1940)
The Leather Pushers (1940)
Give Us Wings (1940)
The Bank Dick (1940)
Meet the Chump (1941)
Buck Privates (1941)
The Invisible Woman (1941)
Six Lessons from Madame La Zonga (1941)
Mr. Dynamite (1941)
In the Navy (1941)
Tight Shoes (1941)
San Antonio Rose (1941)
Hold That Ghost (1941)
Hit the Road (1941)
Too Many Blondes (1941)
Hellzapoppin' (1941)
The Strange Case of Dr. Rx (1942)
Butch Minds the Baby (1942)
Mississippi Gambler (1942)
Private Buckaroo (1942)
Pittsburgh (1942)
Arabian Nights (1942)
Keep 'em Slugging (1943)
It Ain't Hay (1943)
How's About It? (1943)
Strictly in the Groove (1943)
Crazy House (1943)
Moonlight and Cactus (1944)
Strange Affair (1944)
Three of a Kind (1944)
Blondie Knows Best (1946)
Dangerous Business (1946)
The Gentleman Misbehaves (1946)
One Exciting Week (1946)
Africa Screams (1949)

JOE BESSER
Hot Steel (1940)
Africa Screams (1949)
Woman In Hiding (1950)
The Desert Hawk (1950)
Say One for Me (1959)
Let's Make Love (1960)

JOE DeRITA
The Doughgirls (1944)
The Bravados (1958)

Index